COLD PLACES

COLD PLACES

Morgan Llywelyn

POOLBEG

Published in 1995
by Poolbeg Press Ltd
123 Baldoyle Industrial Estate,
Dublin 13, Ireland
Reprinted March 1996

© Morgan Llywelyn 1995

The moral right of the author has been asserted.

A catalogue record for this book is available from the British Library.

ISBN 1 85371 541 7

Cover illustration by Jane Doran
Cover design by Poolbeg Group Services Ltd
Set by Poolbeg Group Services Ltd in Palatino
Printed by The Guernsey Press Company Ltd,
Vale, Guernsey, Channel Islands.

Note on the author

Morgan Llywelyn was born in New York City to parents of Irish and Welsh extraction. A prolific writer of adult books, her books for children include *Brian Boru* and *Strongbow*, winner of the Bisto Award and the Reader's Association of Ireland Award. *Cold Places* is her first novel for Poolbeg.

For Lauren and Brian

Contents

CHAPTER ONE

The last day of school before the summer break was David's favourite day of the year. The whole season stretched before him, his to spend as he liked.

Except this year. This year everything had gone wrong.

"I was rather hoping we might take a holiday in Spain at last," his mother had said as she dusted her collection of china dogs. "We need it after such a cold wet winter. But of course that's not possible now." Sounding more angry than regretful, she flapped the dust cloth hard enough to endanger the fragile figurines.

"Then why can't we stay in Dublin?" David wanted to know. "That's what I want, it's what we usually do anyway."

"You're practically a man now, fifteen-years-old," said his father, glancing up from some papers he was grading at the table by the window. "It's time you understood that people can't always do what they want. I might like a holiday in Spain myself but I need to work."

David replied, "Why can't you go work in Cork, then, and leave us here? You could always come home weekends."

His mother put down her dusting cloth. "Because we're a family, David," Alice McHugh said very firmly. "At least we're supposed to be one." She shot a meaningful look at her husband. There had been a lot of meaningful looks lately. There were shadowy undercurrents in the house, David could sense them. Like clouds gathering. "So we all go to Cork," she went on, "while your father gathers material for his book." She did not sound very happy about it either.

That book! It was taking over their lives, David thought. Because his father was writing a book about archaeological sites in West Cork, they were going to spend the whole summer in a remote place called Bally-Go-Backwards or something. No friends, no chippers, no cinema, just miles and miles of empty countryside. What sort of a summer would that be?

David was bored already.

"I don't see why . . . " he began again at dinner.

Arthur McHugh said with tired patience, "I've explained it to you before. There have been some exciting discoveries around Clonakilty and Rosscarbery and I need to study them so I can

2

include them in my book." Looking up from his meal, he caught his wife's eyes as if he was also speaking to her. "This book could make a big difference to my career."

His wife gave a sniff and looked away.

Some career, thought David. An archaeology professor. Other kids' fathers worked in offices or drove lorries or sold things. Other kids were going to have a good summer, not be stuck out in some remote place where they didn't know anybody.

"Sure," David said aloud. "Great." He tried to sound as if he meant it.

Watching her two men together Alice McHugh observed, not for the first time, how much they resembled one another. David was already almost as tall as his father, with the same dark hair and grave blue eyes. He was thinner, though, whipcord lean. He was a contradiction; a shy, reserved youngster brimming with physical energy he did not know how to spend. She did not understand him any better than she understood her husband. She had met Arthur when she was taking a course on Literature in university, and had once dreamed they would share a lifetime of reading the romantic poets together. Now all the romance in her life was on the telly, while her husband found his in old ruins.

She sighed. The coming few months might be difficult for all of them.

After dinner David went to his room and gazed

3

moodily at the shelf of books above his bed. For once he did not feel like reading. He picked up his camera, turned it over in his hands, put it down. He enjoyed taking photographs; this summer he had intended to take pictures of . . . Aaah, what difference did it make now?

He looked out the window into the Quinlans' side yard and thought of ringing Paddy, but the phone was probably engaged. Paddy's older sister was always on the phone.

Paddy Quinlan had been given a PC for his birthday two weeks earlier. David had looked forward to playing video games with him this summer. Paddy had some great ones, full of action. Pow, bang, splat!

What sort of action would there be in West Cork? Did they even have telly in West Cork?

When he asked that question next morning at breakfast, his father smiled. "Of course they have telly, son. West Cork isn't the end of the world, you know. We're renting a house with all mod cons, as the estate agent says. A lovely country cottage for your mother," he stressed, glancing at his wife. "And I'm sure you'll make some new friends, there are bound to be kids your age in the area."

New friends. The very idea of having to make new friends made David uncomfortable. He liked things the way they were, with his old friends.

"I wish you were staying here, Dav," Paddy said on the morning he went next door to tell him good-bye. They never called each other David and Patrick. Dav was a good nickname, it sounded almost like Dev.

David thought about Dev sometimes, and heroes and the Easter Rising and great adventures. There sure as hell weren't going to be any great adventures in Bally-Go-Backwards.

The McHughs' car was already parked in the street, filled with petrol and ready to go. His father was repacking the boot; his mother was in the front seat, wiping dust off the top of the dash with a tissue. David kept his face turned away from the car.

"So do I," he muttered.

"What are you going to do down there?"

"Watch the fuckin' grass grow, I guess." He and Paddy said fuckin' when they were together, but never when their parents could hear them. Fuckin' was a Dublin word. What did kids say in West Cork?

Paddy grinned. He had a face full of freckles and a gap between his teeth and they had been pals since they were three years old. "I'll think about you while I'm playing *Doom*."

"You don't have *Doom* on your machine!"

"Not now, but I might get it. My dad sorta promised," Paddy boasted.

"David, we're waiting!" his mother's voice called.

With his hands thrust deep in his pockets, David slouched toward the car.

"Bye!" Paddy called.

"Yeah. Sure." Opening the rear door, he climbed in and slammed the door harder than he should have done. His mother looked around sharply. "Day-vid," she said in that tone of voice.

"Sorry." He stared out the window and watched the familiar neighbourhood slide away. Going . . . going . . . gone.

The drive to Cork was a long one, and David riding in the back seat was fighting carsickness, though he would not admit it. When they stopped for lunch he drank a mineral but could not make himself eat anything.

"Day-vid," his mother said again, warningly.

"Sorry, Mom, I'm just not hungry."

"No wonder you don't have a pick on you."

David did not answer. Who cared if he ate or not? His parents were wrapped up in their own thoughts. His father concentrated on the road, drumming his fingers on the steering wheel the way he did sometimes. His mother switched the radio from station to station so fast no one could hear anything all the way through.

In the back seat David tried to think of something to think about.

Gazing out the window, he watched the scenery. There was sure plenty of it. Fields and more fields. Farms, villages, narrow country roads with more potholes than cars. They drove on and on.

Professor McHugh pointed out an abandoned tower house on the horizon, a dark monolith with gaping window holes and part of one wall fallen away. David thought of asking his father to stop so he could take a picture, but the camera was tucked away inside the luggage in the boot. Then Professor McHugh began talking about the history of tower houses in general and David stopped listening. When his father was in lecture mode his ears just seemed to close on their own.

In the front seat his mother yawned. "Arthur, can't you ever talk about anything else?"

"Such as?"

"I don't know. Anything!"

When Professor McHugh made no reply, his wife turned her back on him and stared out the window.

The sky, which had been a radiant blue when they left Dublin, was filling with clouds. At first they were white and puffy like huge mounds of mashed potatoes, and David began to regret that he had not eaten lunch. Then the quality of the light changed and the sky turned dark and ominous. Although it was warm in the car, David felt a shiver run through him. A spatter of rain hit the windscreen. His father turned on the wipers. "I knew the weather was too good to last," he said.

CHAPTER TWO

The family had dinner that night in a restaurant on the outskirts of Cork City. David's parents did not have much to say to each other. While they were waiting for the bill, Arthur McHugh took a folded sheet of paper from his pocket and studied it thoughtfully. "We have quite a way to go yet, and I'm not certain about finding this place after dark."

"Then let's stay in a hotel in Cork City tonight," his wife said promptly.

"A hotel? That would be awfully expensive. Surely we can find a nice B & B. One you'll like, Alice."

But there was a row over the B&B. Every one they went to had something wrong with it, according to Mrs. McHugh. Meanwhile it was getting later and later. When at last they found a place she would accept, David found it hard to go to sleep in a strange bed. Rain lashed against the

8

windows of his room. "I'll bet it isn't raining at home," he muttered to no one in particular.

In the morning it was still raining and the inside of the car smelled damp. After they left the B&B they drove for miles along one narrow, winding road and then another, among heathered hills where great rocks broke through the surface of the land. More than once David's father had to slam on the brakes to avoid a sheep in the road.

At last they stopped beside a rusty iron gate with a low stone wall on either side. Beyond the gate, a narrow, rutted laneway ran through billows of gorse. "Here we are," David's father said with forced cheerfulness. "Open the gate for us, will you, son?"

There was no lock on the gate, just wire twisted around to hold it shut. The rain had finally stopped but the wire was wet and slippery. As David struggled with it he was aware of his parents watching from the car.

Then he realised someone else was watching too.

A girl on a red bicycle had pulled up just behind the car, a tall girl of about his own age. She was wearing jeans and a waxed jacket and had a long plait of sandy hair slung over one shoulder. After a moment she leaned her bike against the wall and came toward him.

"You have to turn it like this," she explained, giving the wire a deft twist. In a moment more she had shoved the gate open.

David was embarrassed. "I was getting it."

"You were making it tighter," she contradicted, but then she smiled. Her smile was as sunny as the skies were dark, and her eyes were a warm, bright blue. "I'm Molly Doyle," she said. "I live up the road, the farm at the head of the valley. Are you the people who've rented the Flanagans' cottage for the summer?"

"I guess so," replied David. "My father teaches at university and we're . . ." Then he noticed his father gesturing to him impatiently from the car. "I, uh, have to go now. 'Bye." He got into the car, feeling his ears burn red.

His mother asked, "Who is that girl, David?"

"She lives on some farm. At the head of the valley," he added as his father put the car in gear and drove slowly through the open gate. The girl waved, then closed the gate after them. When David looked out the rear window she had mounted her bike and was pedalling away.

"At the head of the valley?" mused his father aloud. "I wonder if that's the place where . . . ah, there's the cottage."

"Oh," said Mrs. McHugh in a small, tight voice.

The cottage was shabby and dismal, though its rundown appearance was partially disguised by a riot of climbing roses. Inside, the "mod cons" included a kitchen sink with a blocked drain and a bathtub so stained with rust that David's mother announced she could not possibly sit in that awful thing.

"You insisted on coming," her husband pointed out, "to check up on me."

"I thought it would be better than this!" she said with a sharp glance at David to see if he had heard his father's accusation.

The boy stared at the wall.

"Not on my wages, Alice."

"Your wages." The words were sheathed in ice.

There was going to be an argument, David could feel it. There were too many arguments. Too many raised voices, slammed doors, frosty silences. The frosty silences were the worst, they made him feel helpless. He went out to the car and brought in his things, but he did not stay in the house. Instead he wandered around outside with his hands in his pockets.

Through the open front door he could hear them quarrelling. Then an interior door slammed, followed by a silence as heavy as stone.

David turned his back on the house and walked away.

Beyond the cottage was a broken fence with a stile. Climbing the splintery wooden stile, David found himself in a field overgrown with wildflowers and weeds. A narrow path meandered through tall grass and he followed it. Once or twice he glanced back toward the house, but he kept going.

The path led up a low hill. At the summit he found himself gazing along a crescent-shaped valley through which a silvery stream flowed. At the head of the valley was a big farmhouse and a rather dilapidated barn, and in the distance, something that looked like a circle of stones.

At the moment David saw them another of those peculiar shivers ran across his shoulders.

He turned and headed back toward the cottage. By the time he got there the argument was over, though a sour feeling lingered in the air.

Arthur McHugh greeted his son with a smile that looked pasted on. "What do you think?"

"It's okay."

"I mean, I know the house isn't very posh, but this is the country, it will be fun. Like camping out."

"Sure," said David. His mother, he knew, hated camping out.

That night he found it even harder to sleep than the night before. The quiet of the country had a weight that pressed upon him. He was too aware of the lack of city sounds. Everything was different, strange.

When at last he did fall asleep, the dream came.

CHAPTER THREE

He was standing in a meadow. Grass rippled around him like waves of the sea. Directly in front of him was a circle of standing stones. He knew what they were, his father talked about standing stones often enough. He could see these very clearly. They were dark, rough-textured, crudely hewn. Without any conscious decision on his part, his feet began walking toward them.

As he approached, the stones started to hum.

David awoke in a cold sweat.

At breakfast his father suggested, "Would you like to come with me this morning for a look-round before I get down to work, David? Bring your camera, take some pictures?"

David didn't answer.

"What are you going to do today, Alice?" Arthur McHugh asked his wife.

"Try and rid this house of the smell of mildew," she snapped.

At that moment David made up his mind. "I'll go with you," he told his father. "I'll get the camera."

"And your wellies," Mrs. McHugh insisted although the sun was shining for once.

The day promised to be warm. David thought he would need no more than jeans and a short-sleeved shirt, but he threw a jumper in the back of the car just in case, together with his wellingtons.

As they drove down the laneway from the cottage, David's father said in a low, almost embarrassed, voice, "I know this isn't your mother's idea of a perfect holiday, son. But I'm glad you're coming with me. I'll show you something very interesting." He stopped the car at the closed gate.

"Stone circles?" asked David. The gate made him think of Molly Doyle and the farm in the valley.

Arthur McHugh gave his son a surprised glance. "What makes you ask that?"

"I don't know."

"Well, as it happens, stone circles are just what we're going to see. The best preserved example in the area is near here, it's one reason I took the cottage. There are quite a few ring forts nearby too, and the ruins of a castle, but this circle is special. Last summer a colleague of mine got permission to do a limited dig and found a few artefacts, but more importantly . . ."

David's attention wandered. Professor McHugh

went on talking about carbon dating and Stone versus Bronze Age, but David had stopped listening. He knew his father hoped he would study archaeology someday, but he just could not get interested. Old ruins, scraps of rusting metal, bits of broken pottery. How could they be anything but dull?

He jumped out and opened the gate, being careful to close it afterward and twist the wire back.

"You did that like a real country man," his father commented when he got back in the car.

Although the Doyle farm was just over a hill, to reach it they had to drive down several roads. At last they arrived at another farm gate. This one was freshly painted, however, and standing ajar.

"They're probably expecting us," David's father said. "I made arrangements earlier to view the site."

To David's disappointment, there was no sign of Molly. A weathered farmer who introduced himself as Liam Doyle met them outside the house and gave his father directions for reaching the stone circle. "You'll have to walk, though," he said. "There's no road past the barn. You can park the car there."

David was glad his mother had made him bring his wellies. The earth was sodden. They set off across a mucky field studded with black and white cows who stared at them curiously.

"What if there's a bull?" asked David, wondering if they were about to have an adventure.

Wondering what you did when a bull attacked you.

"Hazards of the profession," his father replied. Then he winked to reassure David there was no bull in the field.

To his surprise, David was beginning to enjoy himself. The air smelled of cattle muck, a pungent odour he would forever after associate with the country. Striding with his father across the field was like being two men together. He did not recall ever having seen his father wink before, or hearing him whistle cheerily as he did now.

At home Arthur McHugh was a quiet man who hid behind textbooks and papers and moved carefully to avoid breaking his wife's knickknacks.

The stone circle was farther from the farmyard than David had thought. As they approached, he was relieved to see that it was not much like the circle in his dream.

A number of grey stones comprised the circle, but the site was somewhat overgrown with thorn trees and brambles, making it difficult to count them. Perhaps half of the stones stood upright, though a few leaned at angles which suggested they would eventually fall over. Others had already fallen and lay in the deep grass.

Before David and his father reached the circle they came upon a large, round-topped boulder lying by itself some yards away. Unlike the other stones, this one was a light golden-brown colour. Professor McHugh paused to remove a notebook from his pocket and began taking notes. ". . . Due east of the entrance to the circle . . . " David heard him muttering to himself as he wrote.

While he waited for his father to finish, the boy examined the far side of the solitary stone. When he looked close he could see what appeared to be strange symbols carved into the surface. There were tiny glittery bits that looked like mica as well. He took his camera from his pocket and fiddled with the light adjustment.

Photographing the figures in the stone was difficult. They were very worn and there was not enough contrast between light and shadow to make them stand out clearly.

"What are you doing, David?"

"I think I found something. Look at these."

Professor McHugh came around the stone and bent over beside him, peering intently.

"Are these manmade symbols?" David wondered.

"Possibly." His father sounded doubtful, however. "But you must remember that stones acquire peculiar characteristics over the ages. Images that look like carving are often the result of weathering, and I would say that is true here." Closing his notebook, he headed for the circle.

David took one final snap, then trotted after him.

A deeply worn path like a cattle track led between two of the stones and into the heart of the circle. Professor McHugh was already inside. He grinned at his son as the boy came toward him, then the grin faded.

"David! What's wrong?"

The boy had come to an abrupt stop between the two pillar stones that marked the entrance. His face was drained of colour and the skin had drawn so tight across his cheekbones that it looked like a skull. Gooseflesh pimpled his bare arms.

Although he stood in radiant sunshine, his teeth were chattering with cold.

CHAPTER FOUR

Arthur McHugh hurried toward his son and put an arm around the boy. David did not even seem to notice. His eyes were fixed and staring.

"David? David!"

He seemed to be very far away. He felt as if he were in some cold, dark place, almost like a cave. He was aware of his father, but only dimly. He did not feel his touch and his voice sounded very faint. All David could really hear was a strange ringing sound that seemed to buzz through his bones.

Cold. He was so very cold. His whole body felt . . . *clenched*. Like a fist. He was waiting for something but he did not know what. Until it happened he could not move, or speak.

David's father half-carried his son to the centre of the circle. As they moved away from the pillar stones David felt warmth flow back into his body. He blinked; shook his head. The world came back into focus and he found his father regarding him anxiously.

"Speak to me, David!"

"I'm okay."

"Are you sure? I thought you were about to faint. Were you in pain?"

David tried to remember. "No, just awfully cold."

"It was more than that, son. As you passed between those two standing stones, suddenly your face looked like a skull. I've never seen anything like it."

David replied, "I didn't feel anything except cold, like I told you." He did not mention the faraway feeling because he did not know how to put it into words. It seemed a very private thing, a secret he wanted to keep for himself. At least for now.

"Are you certain you're all right?"

"Sure."

"Then let's try an experiment. Come over here with me, son, and walk between those stones again, will you?"

They returned to the pillar stones. When he was still a stride away David felt the cold. As he stepped forward it became intense and the faraway feeling returned. His ears began to ring, his body started to clench. But he could see his father waiting for him on the other side of the two stones and he forced himself to keep walking.

Professor McHugh met him with a clap on the shoulder. "That's it lad, well done! But just look at your arms."

Glancing down, David saw the gooseflesh pimpling his forearms. But even as his father led him away from the stones it faded, as did the intense cold. By the time they were four or five paces from the stones all traces were gone.

His father was tremendously excited. He had David repeat the experiment several times, moving close to the stones and then away from them. Next he walked the boy around the circle, trying him with different stones. None of them caused the same effect. But when they moved away from the circle onto open ground, David crossed another patch where he felt sudden, overwhelming cold. Again he found he could move into and out of the cold, almost as if it were a room.

"I think you must be a kind of sensitive, David!" his father enthused. "A bit like a water dowser except your gift involves standing stones, or the region around the stones. You're making a connection with them like closing an electric circuit. Does it feel like that, do you feel a jolt running through you?"

"Not exactly," said the boy, trying to remember more clearly. His father's excitement was beginning to infect him too.

"And your face! And the gooseflesh on your arms! It's all part of the same thing. We have to talk to someone about this. But first I would like to try you at a couple of other sites to see if the phenomenon occurs elsewhere or just here. You wouldn't mind, would you?"

"I guess not." David could not remember ever doing anything that pleased his father so much as this.

At that moment the sky darkened and the sun vanished behind a bank of swiftly racing cloud. "We'd better get back to the cottage for now," Arthur McHugh said. He grinned like a boy as he added, "I'll race you to the car!"

Laughing, happy, they ran back across the fields as the first raindrops spattered on their faces.

However when they returned to the cottage and related the morning's adventure to David's mother, her eyes flashed with anger. "How could you treat a sick child like that!" she demanded of her husband.

"I was not ill," David tried to explain. "I just felt funny for a minute, Mom. It was strange, that's all."

"You were ill," she told him emphatically. "And it's typical of your father to put his own interests above yours."

"It was only a harmless experiment, Alice. And you heard the lad yourself, he wasn't . . ."

"Look at him, Arthur! He's as pale as a ghost. David, you go lie down this very minute. I'll bring you some tea and toast later on – after I finish talking to your father."

Through the closed door of his bedroom David could hear raised voices again. At least he could hear his mother's raised voice. His father was quieter. It was a row, though. He could always tell.

22

Lying on his bed, listening to the rain drumming on the roof, he thought about what had happened at the stone circle. It was mysterious and exciting and a little bit frightening; his first brush with the unknown.

The Unknown. He whispered the word to himself. Paddy would be so jealous when he told him! It was like seeing a ghost or something.

He looked forward eagerly to the next day, when they would visit other ancient sites and test his response again.

But his mother was set against it. "You are not dragging this child out to use him like a laboratory animal," Alice McHugh told her husband next morning.

"I want to go," David insisted. "And I'm not a child, I'm fifteen."

"There's no harm can come to him. All that happens is he feels cold, he'll tell you himself." His father did not, David noticed, remind his wife what he had said earlier, about David having gooseflesh and his face resembling a skull.

Mrs. McHugh kept arguing. Listening to the two of them, David became convinced that the quarrel wasn't really about him at all, but about other issues.

At last his mother gave an elaborate shrug. "Take him then, if you're so determined. Why should you listen to me?"

A muscle twitched in her husband's jaw. "Maybe

that's the trouble, maybe I've listened to you too much. I've given in to you on just about everything since we got married. I'm up to my ears in debt. But you can't always have it your own way, Alice."

"I let you have your way, didn't I? I let you stay late at university without asking who you were with, and I came to this wretched place with you."

"You insisted on coming because . . . " He stopped, glanced at his son as if he had just remembered the boy was in the room. "Come on, David," he said abruptly.

"Take a jacket!" Alice McHugh ordered. "It isn't as warm as it was yesterday."

David grabbed a jacket and followed his father outside. Arthur McHugh slammed the car door very hard. Only after they had driven to the foot of the lane and through the gateway did David remember he had come off without his camera. But he did not ask his father to go back.

They drove in silence for a little while. The car felt thick with tension. A dark sky promised a return of the rain. Then just ahead of them they saw a girl on a red bike. "There's Molly Doyle!" David cried. "Can we ask her to come with us?"

His father hesitated. "We aren't playing games, son."

"I know that. But you said I should make new friends."

Professor McHugh looked at his son's face. Then his own expression softened. "All right, but I want

24

you to concentrate on what we're doing. It might be important."

"I know. And thanks." David leaned out the car window. "Molly! Hi!"

Molly appeared glad to see him, and when he explained that they were going to look at some ancient stones – "Field monuments," his father interjected – she agreed to join them. They put her bike in the boot and held the lid down with bunjee cords.

"I used to play in that stone circle on our farm when I was a little girl," Molly said from the back seat as the car started up again.

"Did you ever . . . feel anything funny there?" David wanted to know.

"Funny how?"

He explained as best he could what had happened the day before. She seemed as intrigued as he was. "I'm glad I'm coming with you. I'd like to see that myself!"

"You won't be scared?"

"Scared!" She burst out laughing.

David liked having Molly with them. She was sunny and happy and smelled like fresh country air. Usually he was shy with new people, but he had felt comfortable with Molly from the beginning.

His father stopped once more to consult a small map, then eventually turned into a narrow laneway. "Here we are," he announced.

David looked in the direction his father was pointing. On a hillside above the lane stood a great slab of stone with one end propped on two smaller stones. The moment he saw it David felt the now-familiar shiver run along his spine.

CHAPTER FIVE

Professor McHugh separated two strands of wire and climbed through the fence into the field. "Come on!" he called. "I'll hold the wire for you." David eased between the strands and then held them in turn for Molly.

As they walked up the slope his father was explaining, "What you will be seeing is known as a boulder dolmen. This one is aligned to the southwest, and happens to be in an almost straight line with three other field monuments in the area, all featuring the same alignment."

David tried to catch Molly's eye and fake a yawn. But to his surprise, Molly was gazing at Professor McHugh with obvious interest. "Just what are dolmens?" the girl asked him.

"An early form of tomb," he replied. "Originally they were probably covered with earth and pebbles to form a chamber within a mound, but over thousands of years the covering has worn away.

Now only the big capstones and their supports remain. Megalithic monuments date from the Stone Age, but later Bronze Age burials have been found in a number of them. This one has not been excavated, so we don't know just what . . . " He stopped in midsentence to stare at David.

The boy was standing perfectly still some thirty feet from the dolmen. All the colour had drained from his face.

"What is it?" his father asked.

But David could barely hear him. He was on the same windswept hillside and yet it was not the same. For one thing, he was suddenly, bitterly cold. He was also aware of a number of other people around him but he could not see them. Yet he felt the presence of their shadowy forms moving back and forth, and at the edge of his consciousness he heard a sound like keening.

The forms were clustering around the patch of ground on which he stood. They were digging in the earth, he could *feel* them doing it. They were burying something . . .

"David!" his father exclaimed, shaking him.

"It's here," the boy cried, suddenly dropping to his knees and beginning to scrabble at the earth. "Right here!"

"What? What's here?"

David looked up at his father, speechless. With his hands he made shapes. At last he blurted, "They buried their offerings *here*."

There was no telephone back at the cottage, so Professor McHugh drove on to the nearest village. During the drive he asked his son several times, "Are you sure, David? Are you certain?" When they reached the village he sent David and Molly into the pub to order a pub lunch for the three of them while he rang the University of Cork. When David went outside to the phone kiosk to get his father he heard him saying, "I tell you, Charlie, the boy has a remarkable response to these things. It may just be nonsense, but I think it's worth taking a look." Seeing David, he winked at his son.

David felt immensely proud.

Over their lunch Professor McHugh said, "A friend of mine from the archaeology department at UCC will be coming out as soon as he has the time. He's arranging permission for us to conduct a very small exploratory dig at that site, just in case there *is* anything there."

"Can we watch?" asked David.

"I definitely want you there, son. You have some sort of gift; a racial memory perhaps. Something you have inherited in your blood from your earliest ancestors. There is a quote from W. B. Yeats . . . " his voice assumed lecturing mode again," . . . that many minds can flow into one another and create or reveal a single mind, a single energy. And that our memories are part of one great memory, the memory of nature herself."

"Yeats was a famous Irish poet," David explained to Molly.

She stuck out her tongue at him. "I know that. Everybody knows that!"

As they drove back, he could not resist teasing her by asking, "Did your parents not warn you about getting into a car with strangers?"

"You aren't strangers, you're our neighbours. Besides, this is the country. Nothing much ever happens here. You live in Dublin, that's ever so much more exciting. And archaeologists go to wonderful places, don't they? Greece and Rome and places?"

Professor McHugh's lips twitched. "Sometimes," he responded. "Some do."

"That must be great. I never get to see anything interesting."

"You saw that dolmen today."

"I see things like that all the time," said Molly. "But today is the only time there's been anything exciting about them."

"They're always exciting if you think about them as clues to a giant puzzle, Molly. Or better yet, keys that can open doors," David's father went on. "One of the last frontiers on earth is the past. Archaeology is about exploring that frontier, so every scrap of information we find is important. Every surviving trace from man's ancient past has a story to tell us. For that matter, some scientists believe that everything that ever happened on this planet is recorded in vibrations that still exist in the stones, like books waiting to be read."

David looked back at Molly. Her eyes were huge. "Is that true?" she asked him as if he were as knowledgeable as his father.

"Maybe."

"I know other places where there are, uh, dolmens, and ancient stones and things. Would you like me to show you where they are?"

"We already have maps of all the field monuments in the area," Professor McHugh said, but Molly laughed.

"I'll bet I know places that aren't on any map."

David's father frowned. "*Amateurs*," he replied, stressing the word, "often think something is an important monument when it's only field clearance."

Molly sniffed. "I know what field clearance is. My father takes stones out of his fields all the time and piles them up. I'm not talking about that."

It occurred to David that his father was reluctant to admit a country girl might know something a university professor did not.

Once, he remembered, he had thought his father knew everything. He had thought his father was the wisest man in the world and his mother was the best cook and could quote all sorts of poetry and life would always go on as it was. Safe and predictable.

He wanted it to be safe and predictable. Or did he?

31

CHAPTER SIX

They drove Molly back to the farm because the rain had begun again. "I'll see you tomorrow," she promised David as he helped her unload her bike from the boot.

That afternoon Professor McHugh busied himself with writing up his notes and consulting various textbooks he had brought with him. David roamed restlessly around the cottage for a while, then put on his jacket and went outside.

"You'll catch your death!" his mother called after him but he pretended not to hear.

The rain had given way to a soaking mist that lay like a weight on his face as he rambled along the lane. The countryside appeared deserted and the afternoon was very quiet; unnaturally so to a boy from the city. David stepped through a gap in a wall, crossed a field, then another. The earth smelled wet and mucky, but it was not an unpleasant smell. Sharp. And natural. Not like motor exhaust.

A bird sang in a great clump of gorse. Smiling to himself, David wandered on. He had no idea where he was going except anything was better than staying inside with his parents.

Then all at once he felt it again. He stopped abruptly.

A cold place lay right in front of him.

When he looked down there was nothing to see but boggy earth, deeply cupped where cattle had cut up the ground with their hooves. Yet there was something invisible but very tangible in that place. David felt certain he could touch it if he reached out his hand.

He walked in a slow, careful circle, exploring the boundaries of the cold place without ever stepping all the way inside. He found it had definite dimensions. The entire area was no more than eight feet long by perhaps six feet wide. He made a second circle then stopped at one end, drew a deep breath, and took a step forward.

The cold clutched him like a fist. At the same moment his stomach seemed to swoop downward. He had a terrifying sensation of falling, the earth dropping out from under him, himself tumbling into some cold alien darkness with no getting back . . .

David tried to scream but no sound came out. He clawed at the air, struggling to keep his balance. Cold and dark and death were all around him. Not death, really . . . but an absence of life. He was in the lair of a monster that hated all things warm and living and sucked the life out of them. If he surrendered he would be swallowed up and become part of the nothingness.

Though he did not know what he was fighting, he fought back. But his muscles were no use. His fists had no power against the darkness and the cold. He could only fight with his mind, concentrating on images of his parents and Paddy and his other friends . . . and Molly Doyle. Warm living people!

He locked his thoughts on them and reached out, clutching desperately . . .

The monster roared. Its cold breath burned through him like icy flame.

Then the terror faded. He found himself standing in a muddy field. Alone. Alive.

David could not bring himself to go back to the cottage and face his mother's questions. Instead he made the much longer walk to the Doyles' farm. Molly was surprised to see him looking cold and miserable on the doorstep, but took him inside at once. She led the way to a big, warm kitchen and sat him down in front of the Aga. Before he said anything she insisted on making him a cup of cocoa.

The hot drink tasted wonderful. He savoured its warmth spreading through him. Rousing himself a little, he looked around the kitchen. "Where's your mother?"

"I'm mother," Molly replied matter-of-factly. "I

mean, I do the cooking and cleaning and washing up. My Mam, God have mercy on her, died when I was little."

"Oh, I'm sorry!"

"So were we," the girl replied softly. Then she brightened. "Now, do you feel better?"

"I do."

She sat down beside him at the kitchen table. "What happened? You were awfully pale just now on the doorstep."

His description of the experience in the field was confused and incomplete. The things he had felt were hard to put into words. But he did his best.

"How exciting!" cried Molly when he finished. "Nothing like that ever happens to me." She jumped up and refilled David's mug.

As the steam from the cocoa rose, warming his face, David recalled the cold. The terrible cold. "It was like falling into my own grave, Molly," he said with a shudder.

She decided to change the subject. She found it both fascinating and intriguing, but it might be best for him to talk about something else for a while. "Tell me, David – do you go to discos in Dublin?"

"Discos? Ah . . . sure. I mean . . . well, I did once." He did not add that his mother disapproved of discos and he and Paddy had sneaked in to one.

"What was it like?" the girl asked eagerly.

Thinking about the disco made the cold place seem far away, unreal. It could not compete with a memory of flashing lights and loud music and gyrating bodies. He described the disco in detail for Molly, making up parts where his knowledge failed. She took it all in with wide eyes. "I would love to go to a disco," she said, "but we don't have any around here."

"If you come up to Dublin sometime I'll take you to one," David promised.

They continued to talk, unaware of time passing. He began to feel embarrassed for having been so frightened. He did not want Molly to think he was a wimp. "Maybe I just had food poisoning or something," he said at last to explain his experience. "I'm okay now, really."

"Are you sure?"

David was tired of people asking him if he was all right. "Of course I am!" he insisted. He even winked at Molly the way his father winked at him, to convince her he was in good form.

By the time he left the Doyles' farm and made his way back to the cottage, he really was feeling much better. He had enjoyed an adventure and Molly admired him for it. No harm was done.

In fact, he was beginning to think of himself as someone special.

The rain had stopped, though he could still smell it on the wind. But he was not cold and his earlier fear seemed like the imaginings of a child.

CHAPTER SEVEN

When the archaeologist from the university arrived, Professor McHugh introduced him as "a colleague of mine, Charlie Ryan." He did not mention their plans to his wife, merely bundled Professor Ryan and David into the car and set off.

"I thought you said Molly could go with us," David protested.

His father gave him an absent-minded glance. "Next time, son."

Charles Ryan was a stocky, muscular man, younger than David had expected. As they drove he did not mention archaeology at all but admitted to following Manchester United and talked knowledgeably about football.

Then the conversation switched to the weather. "Worst I've ever seen," Professor Ryan said. "Rain, fog, drizzle, frost – what's gone wrong, Bill?"

"I don't know," David's father replied. "We had an appalling winter in Dublin. Ah, here we are."

He pulled into the laneway below the boulder dolmen.

Suddenly both men were all business. Shouldering canvas carryalls filled with equipment, they strode purposefully up the hill. David's father turned back and called, "Are you not coming, son? We need you to show us exactly where to dig."

Feeling important, David hurried after them.

He was not certain he could find the place again, yet he had no difficulty. It drew him almost like a magnet. "Here," he called. "Right here, this is the spot."

The cold reached out to him.

He did not stand on the actual place but waited at one side, pointing. He had no desire to set foot on that particular piece of earth again. But the two archaeologists had no hesitation. Nor did they seem to feel anything unusual as they squatted down and began brushing through the grass with their hands, examining the soil beneath.

Then Professor Ryan removed a camera from his carryall and photographed the site from every angle. Meanwhile Professor McHugh made a number of measurements. Only then did the archaeologists begin their dig. They scraped the soil away by millimetres, using small trowels, spatulas, spoons, even soft brushes. Occasionally they paused to take more pictures and make more notes.

The process was dreadfully slow and the men seemed to forget all about David. They did not notice when he drifted away. He climbed the hill to the dolmen, where he took his own camera from his pocket and used up all the film in it taking pictures of the ancient tomb.

There was no cold place at the dolmen.

Time seemed to stand still.

"David!" cried his father at last. "Look here! We've found something."

He ran back down the slope, getting as close as he could without actually entering the zone of cold in which the men were working. Craning his neck, David glimpsed the mud-encrusted metal they were patiently uncovering.

At last Professor Ryan lifted the object out and held it up, almost with reverence, for David to see. The boy's breath caught in his throat.

The find was a gold circlet, twisted into a spiral. Gently rubbing with his thumb, Ryan revealed complex designs cut into the flatter surfaces of the spiral.

"I've never seen anything like this," David's father breathed.

His colleague nodded stunned agreement. "It's older than anything we've found around here, I'm thinking. Look at those patterns! We need to get this to the university as soon as possible, of course, conduct tests . . . it's a spectacular find. We'll be coming back to do a more extended dig."

"You did well, son," Professor McHugh said, clapping David on the back.

Professor Ryan agreed. "If this ability of yours proves to be genuine, you can write your own ticket. I wish I had such a son."

As they walked back to the car Arthur McHugh put his arm around David's shoulders.

They were very late returning to the cottage and Alice McHugh was predictably angry. David went straight to his room to avoid the row. He needed to be alone anyway to sort out his feelings. Finding the gold was the thrill of a lifetime – but he had to admit part of him was scared. Deep down scared.

From the moment the men began digging, he had felt the cold extending. That was why he kept moving away. He had longed to tell them it leave it alone, but he dared not. They would have laughed at him. And how could he explain what he felt when he did not understand it himself?

Arthur McHugh left for Cork City early the next morning without offering to take David with him. David had just begun to feel part of his father's world. Now he was shut out again. He decided to go over to the Doyles' farm and see Molly since there was nothing else to do. Being with her made him feel better about himself.

When he told her about the gold circlet, she was thrilled. "Here!" she kept saying. "Right here!"

"Well, not exactly here."

"You know what I mean, it's practically our back garden. Something exciting at last. *Gold*, David! Can you find more, do you think? Or other things?"

"I don't know."

"Let's go and see. I told you I knew lots of places like that one."

David hesitated. "I'm not sure I want to do this any more."

"Of course you do! Come on!"

She had only the one bike and it was not a mountain bike, so they walked. "Everyone walks in the country," Molly told David. Both were wearing jeans and trainers, and summer weight tee shirts. In addition Molly had knotted a pink cotton cardigan around her waist. "See those clouds?" she said. "It could rain or turn a lot colder."

He shrugged. Boys don't feel the cold, his shrug implied.

She did not lead him toward the stone circle, but in the opposite direction. They walked for a long time and David was surprised that the girl never complained of being tired. He didn't know any girls back home who could walk like that.

And she knew so many things! As they went along she pointed out different birds and told him their names and habits. She knew the names of trees, too, and flowers, and talked without embarrassment about breeding livestock. The world Molly Doyle knew was as foreign to him as the civilisation which had erected the standing stones, and he thought one as exotic as the other.

But Molly was in this one. And she made things fun.

Suddenly David felt a familiar, disturbing sensation. He stopped like a hound scenting a hare. Molly paused beside him. "What is it?"

"Over there." He pointed. "There's something over there."

"That's the fairy fort I was telling you about. Your father calls them ring forts. This one has a couple of big stones on the other side that probably marked the entrance once. Farmers plough fairy forts under sometimes, but they've never touched this one. There are all sorts of stories about it that frighten them off, but I think . . ."

"Don't," said David, his voice barely a whisper. "Don't go over there. Oh please, Molly. *Don't.*"

CHAPTER EIGHT

He could feel the cold even at a distance. The cold, and the terrible, stomach-dropping-out-of-you sensation. Without being aware of it, he began to step backward.

But Molly caught him by the arm. "Oh come on, David, it isn't really a fairy fort. There's no evil spell on it or anything. You're from Dublin, you know better than that! Let's go explore it together. It will be fun to try to imagine how people lived there long ago."

She tugged harder. How could he explain to this bright and sunny girl the feelings that were swirling through him?

So he let her lead him toward the earthen embankment.

The bank was a large ring of raised ground on which wild grasses grew. David noticed that there were no shadows. Everything looked two-dimensional. The clouds diffused the light so that no one object stood out more than another.

Yet the ring fort seemed to loom huge before

him. It was larger than he first thought, the banks higher. It was . . . crouching . . . on the earth, waiting for him.

"Come *on*." Molly tugged at his arm again, then turned him loose and raced off toward the fort, running lightly up the sloping bank to the top. From that vantage point she looked down at him and grinned. "It's great up here. You can see for miles."

As he had made himself walk between the two pillar stones to reach his father, now David made himself climb the bank to Molly. Every step of the way he grew colder. A faint, far-off ringing sounded in his ears, like tiny crystal bells. Like icicles.

He reached the top of the bank and stood beside Molly, looking around at the ring. His sense of perspective was distorted, he could not tell how high up they were or how wide the ring was. One moment he seemed to have climbed no more than eight or ten feet. The next moment the ground was frighteningly far below him.

"I told you you could really see from up here," said Molly's cheerful voice beside him. Or was she beside him? Was she not miles and miles . . . and years and years . . . away?

"Look over there," her voice went on. "What's that, David?"

She was pointing. He followed the direction of her extended forefinger, trying to focus his eyes on something in the distance.

He saw something white that glittered in spite of the sunless skies. A vast expanse of whiteness like a snow-capped mountain range, but there were no mountains. Not in that direction. And not snow-capped in the summer. "I don't know," he said in a hoarse whisper.

Molly made a shelf of her hand over her eyebrows and peered out from under it. "It looks almost like a picture I saw once of a glacier," she said. "But that's not possible, not in Ireland."

"No, not in Ireland," the boy echoed hollowly.

He was cold, so terribly cold! His teeth were beginning to chatter. He turned away from the outward view and looked down into the centre of the ring. For a moment he felt a rush of vertigo that made him sick and dizzy. Then it cleared.

Everything cleared. His vision became very sharp. He could see every detail of grass and stone in the ring fort in stark relief. He could see, between the blades of grass, the brown earth beneath.

And the vast, shapeless bulk of something that lay *under* the earth.

With a cry, David staggered back. He might have tumbled backwards down the slope if Molly had not caught hold of him. "What is it? What's wrong?" she asked anxiously.

His mouth was so dry he could not form words.

"Here, sit down. You've gone all pale again. David, are you ill?"

He managed to shake his head. "I'm not ill." He was embarrassed to have her hovering over him. After a moment he made himself get to his feet to show her he was all right. But as soon as he stood up he felt something pulling at him.

Pulling, tugging, drawing . . .

Against his will he began to walk down the side of the embankment to the centre of the ring fort.

"Where are you going now?" called Molly.

He did not answer.

"Wait for me!" she shouted, but he did not even hear.

The force that drew him had him firmly in its grip now. Helplessly, he advanced step by step toward the centre of the ring. As he did so he felt the faraway sensation enveloping him again and his ears began to ring. Then the ground seemed to tilt sideways. He staggered and flung out his arms.

The scene swirled around him. The landscape spun past at a dizzying speed; vanished; re-appeared in different hues, summer gold and autumn brown and winter grey. The light changed and changed again as if the sun were rising and setting every other second. Unseen forces held David fast though he flung his body from side to side and flailed his arms, shouting in a mix of terror and anger. The centre of the ring fort became an arena in which he was fighting for his life.

He tried to concentrate his mind, the only weapon he had. For a moment the grip that held him eased and he thought he could break free. But when a wash of relief broke his concentration he was captured again.

As David watched in horror the grass-covered embankment shimmered and became briefly transparent, then vanished altogether.

Where a green field in high summer had been, all was ice.

Towering peaks of white dazzled the eye. An expanse of ice-sheathed snow stretched in every direction, featureless and trackless. Howling winds swirled around the boy; particles of ice like needles stung his exposed flesh.

The cold was intolerable. When he tried to scream he could only cough as the wind rushed down his throat. It sucked the air from his lungs and turned his warm breath to frost. *This is a nightmare!* he thought, but he knew it was no nightmare. It was something worse – reality.

CHAPTER NINE

Standing atop the embankment, Molly had watched David walk down toward the centre. She could not understand why he did not answer when she called to him. But she ran down after him anyway – then halted abruptly.

Something was terribly wrong.

She could see him just in front of her, but it was as if she were looking at him through a pane of cloudy glass. On the other side of the pane he was throwing himself from side to side and waving his arms wildly. His mouth was open, he seemed to be shouting, but she could not hear what he was saying. And the glass would not let her go to him.

David felt more alone than ever in his life. Reality had shifted around him when he entered the ring fort. Had the fabric of time been torn somehow? He had read horror stories and science fiction about such things, but he never thought they could really happen. Yet it seemed the only explanation. Now he found himself trapped in the grim and cruel Ice Age when elemental forces were reshaping the land. The wind cut through his summer clothing and froze the flesh beneath.

His only hope of staying alive was to keep moving. The force that had captured him did not keep him from jumping up and down and running in place. He began a series of frantic gymnastics to keep himself warm. At the same time he was desperately trying to think. How had this happened? How could he get back to his own time and place?

He could not even see very clearly because the sun shining on the ice created a dazzle that hurt his eyes. But it was not the sun he knew. This sun was without heat, at least without enough heat to warm the terrible landscape. The ice was all-powerful here, and David was its captive.

Molly screamed his name but he did not appear to hear. He was running as hard as he could, yet not going anywhere. She had never seen anyone look so frightened.

The girl was frightened herself by now. She had to get to David somehow, had to break through the invisible barrier between them. If he was having some sort of fit he would need help, but first she had to reach him.

She beat her fists against the invisible barrier and

called his name again and again. He half-turned and she thought he was looking in her direction. "David! *David! Over here!*"

Their eyes met.

In that deadly white landscape there was no movement, no colour, nothing living but himself and he would not be living much longer. David knew he was growing weaker. He gazed wildly around one last time, seeking an escape that was not there, and then he saw . . .

Colour.

Two dots of warm blue in all that icy coldness.

Two big blue eyes staring pleadingly into his!

"Molly!"

The boy flung himself toward those eyes. At the same moment Molly felt the barrier between them waver and become less solid, more like a layer of jelly than of glass. She thrust her arms through it and David fell into them.

Simultaneously there was a terrible roaring sound in the ring fort, as if some monster slumbering far beneath the earth had awakened in agony.

The boy and girl sat side by side on the damp grass, gasping for breath. To her astonishment, Molly realised that David was ice cold. His clothing was frozen stiffly against his body. His face was an abnormal red, almost like the first stages of frostbite, and his lips were cracked and bleeding.

"What happened to you?" she asked when she got her breath back.

He could only shake his head. He was shivering violently.

She knew she had to get him warm. Unknotting the cardigan from around her waist, she pulled it across his shoulders and tried to get his arms into the sleeves. At last he roused himself enough to help her. But he was still shivering.

Without hesitating, Molly wrapped her arms around David and pulled him close against her own warm self.

Gradually he stopped shivering. With a shy, embarrassed smile, she released him and moved a little bit away. "Are you all right now?"

"I think so." His cracked lips hurt when he tried to talk.

She asked again, "What happened?"

With an effort, he tried to explain. As he talked Molly insisted they head for home. The two walked slowly because David was still weak and shaken. By the time they reached the Doyles' farm he had related his adventure as best he could, but there was no way he could make her fully understand just how terrible it was.

"I couldn't get to you," she kept saying.

She invited him to come in and have a mug of hot tea, but suddenly David just wanted to be with his parents. Molly had saved his life, he knew, and he was tremendously grateful. But he was also very badly scared. More than anything he wanted to go home.

Yet he could not go home, he suddenly realised. Home for now was that shabby cottage and his parents bickering.

Seeing the indecision in his eyes, Molly caught him by the hand and tugged him into the farmhouse. She sat him down in the big warm kitchen and gave him mug after mug of tea sweetened with honey until he began to feel better.

As time passed the horror of the Ice Age began to fade a little. He was still frightened by what had happened, but he did not want the girl to know just how scared he had been.

"I had best be going," he said at last.

Looking at him, Molly laughed. "Take off that pink cardigan before your parents see you," she said.

But they would not have noticed. When he reached the cottage his mother was in her bedroom with the door shut. His father was still in Cork.

David went into the bathroom and peered at his reflection in the tarnished mirror over the old-fashioned hand wash basin. Molly had told him his face was red; now he could see for himself what looked like a very bad windburn. When he touched his cheek with his fingertips it felt numb.

His fingers were only slightly less numb, however.

He filled the rusty bathtub with water as hot as he could stand, then sank gratefully into it.

Dinner was late that evening. When Professor McHugh finally came home from the city he was brimming with excitement about the find on the dolmen hill; he did not even notice David's flushed face. The boy's mother had commented on it when she at last emerged from her room, but had accepted his explanation of wind chapping his skin. "You have fragile skin like mine," she said.

There was ice cream for dessert. Vanilla. David stared at the white mound in his bowl, then shuddered and pushed it away.

"I thought you loved ice cream," commented his mother, sounding as if her feelings were hurt. "I got this just for you."

He mumbled, "I'm just too full. If I eat any more I'll be ill."

"We have to take care of you, son," his father said. "A talent like yours . . . do you realise that piece you located is absolutely unique? It's nothing like any other ornament found in Ireland and opens whole new realms of possibility. One of the specialists we were talking to today felt it might be Neolithic or even older, which would make it the oldest known piece of metalwork in . . . "

He went on and on enthusiastically. He was brimming with plans to take David to every ancient site in the area, hoping to locate other finds.

But David had stopped listening. He sat slouched in his chair, trying not to look at the cold, glittering white peak of the ice cream.

CHAPTER TEN

The next few weeks were very strange. Professor McHugh took David with him to a number of places in west Cork. They visited single standing stones and stone circles, hill forts, ring forts, dolmens, wedge tombs – "I never knew there were so many field monuments," David told his father as they were driving to see a carved standing stone of particular interest.

"Ireland is very rich in megalithic sites, son. And they were built over quite a span of time. The first people came here in the Mesolithic, or Middle Stone Age, but many of our most famous monuments, like Newgrange, were erected by Neolithic people. Late Stone Age."

"What about the Ice Age?" David wanted to know. "Who was here then?"

"Ireland was uninhabited as far as we know. Huge glaciers ground their way across the earth, shaping the land into the form it has today. The cold was unimaginable. Seeds survived in the earth under the ice, of course, and when the glaciers finally receded life returned. In time the first Stone Age settlers arrived from elsewhere in Europe."

The boy frowned. "Will the Ice Age ever come back?"

"It might," his father conceded. "Climate change runs in cycles. Ireland has been both colder and warmer than it is now – at different times, of course. And we seem to be entering another period of change. Greenhouse effect or global warming, no one knows for . . . ah, here we are." When he saw his target Professor McHugh forgot all about the Ice Age.

But David could not.

A few, a very few, of the places they visited had cold spots. Sometimes they were close to ancient stones; sometimes they were a distance away. But none of them were as powerful as whatever David had found in the ring fort.

There were other finds, however. Twice he was convinced there was something under the earth, and both times his father and Professor Ryan found valuable artefacts exactly where he said they would. One was a metal ornament of some sort, with a pattern similar to that on the first gold circlet.

With each discovery, more and more archaeologists became involved. Soon there were eight or ten who wanted to accompany David and his father wherever they went. They treated David partly like a celebrity and partly, as he ruefully explained to Molly, "like a freak."

"They talk about me as if I'm not there," he told her. "For a while in the beginning I was excited about this stuff, but now . . ."

"Now?"

"I wish it had never started."

"They can't make you do it, can they?"

"It isn't like that. This means a lot to my father. He says I'm like a dowser, except I find antiquities."

Molly's blue eyes lit up. "I know what a dowser is. When we needed a new well my father sent for a dowser from Clonakilty. He took a forked alder branch and walked across the field carrying it in front of him until all of a sudden it jumped in his hand and pointed down. 'Dig here,' he said. Da did, and there was water, just like magic!"

David nodded. "My father says there are different types of dowsers. Nobody knows just how it works, but he doesn't think it's magic. He says it's a natural phenomenon science doesn't fully understand yet. Some dowsers can locate oil, others find iron, or copper, or even lost objects. They respond to whatever's in the earth, or it calls out to them. There's some sort of a connection between them. He says he's never heard of anyone else who can do what I can, though. He's really proud of me, and that makes me feel good."

"Then I don't see what the problem is," said Molly sensibly.

The problem was . . . David was afraid. Every day he was more afraid. Each time he felt the touch of that alien cold, he remembered being trapped in a world of snow and ice and expecting to die.

He tried to tell himself it was his imagination. Or an hallucination. Or even food poisoning. If he tried to describe it to his parents, that is what they would say. Yet he knew it was real, a totally hostile world lurking just beyond the thinnest of barriers, waiting to come again.

In his dreams at night the Ice Age did return. He had visions of giant icebergs bursting through the earth of grassy meadows. His sleep was haunted by the relentless grinding of glaciers, crushing everything before them. He awoke from his nightmares chilled to the bone with fear.

"You're not eating enough," his mother scolded him. "You're getting thinner and thinner."

"Don't pick on the boy, Alice," said her husband.

"I'm not picking on him! You're the one who keeps him away until all hours. I doubt if you ever think to feed him, you're so . . . "

Now they were quarrelling over him. David couldn't bear it. Whenever he had the chance he fled to the Doyles' farm and spent time with Molly and her father. Liam Doyle was gruff and said little, but he made it obvious he enjoyed having David around the place. Being with them was like summer.

His parents were winter.

Winter was stealing up on him in other ways, too. In the morning, he began finding his fingers and toes numb with cold when he woke up, even though he had slept beneath a duvet.

"I need more blankets for my bed," he told his mother.

Alice McHugh gave her son an appraising look. "It's not more blankets you need, it's more food. Anyone as thin as you feels the cold."

She gave him the blankets, however. Later she complained to her husband about the dampness in the house making David's bedroom cold. "That boy is going to be ill and it's your fault."

"He won't be ill if you'll stop talking about him being ill all the time. You're the one who puts ideas into his head, making him feel sickly."

A new row broke out.

David fled to the Doyle farm. "I hate it when they fight," he told Molly as she opened the door for him.

"Forget it for now, think of something else. What would you like to do?"

David glanced at the sky. Overcast all morning, it was now beginning to spit drops of rain. "I don't know. What can we do in weather like this, watch telly?"

"The reception isn't very good here," she admitted. "But yesterday's newspaper is inside and I haven't read it yet. Would you like to read it with me?"

Reading the newspapers had never been one of David's interests, but suddenly it seemed a very grown-up thing to be doing. Especially with Molly. "Sure," he said.

The two youngsters made themselves comfortable in the kitchen. Molly's father was working on a piece of farm machinery in the shed, clearly visible through the window. Molly rapped on the pane with her knuckles and he glanced up and grinned.

They spread out the Cork paper on the big kitchen table and settled themselves to read. The room smelled of cooking and newsprint and pipe tobacco; warm, homely smells.

David's attention was drawn to a headline which proclaimed: COLDEST SUMMER EVER! As he read on down the article, he learned that the temperature was setting new lows all across Ireland. The cap of winter snow atop Carrauntual had never melted. Unseasonable frost had been reported as far south as Limerick, and drivers in the midlands claimed they had encountered patches of black ice on the roads.

"Listen to this," he told Molly, reading aloud.

The girl was unimpressed. "Irish weather," she said dismissively.

"No, it's more than that. My father thinks the climate's changing."

"It takes thousands of years for the climate to change."

"Maybe it used to," replied David. "It's happening fast now, though."

"Why?"

The boy shook his head. "I don't know. "At that moment something spattered hard against the window and he glanced up. Tiny pellets of ice were striking the glass. "Sleet!"

Molly jumped to her feet. "It can't be."

But it was.

CHAPTER ELEVEN

The weather drove Mr. Doyle inside to get a heavier jacket. As he passed the door of the sitting room he glanced in at the children.

"You ski, lad?" he asked David jokingly.

Somehow it did not seem funny.

The weather did not improve. The sleet gave way to an icy, dismal rain. As the day darkened, Molly turned on the lights. "I had best be getting home," David told her reluctantly.

"You can't go out now, it's pissing rain."

He grinned in spite of himself. "I'll be all right, we have rain in Dublin too and I've never melted yet."

"You might not melt, but you'd freeze. It's gone very cold. Why do you not wait until Da comes back in and we'll ask him to drive you over in the car?"

David didn't need much persuading.

When he returned to the cottage his mother met

him at the door, complaining about the weather. "Turn on the radio," he suggested, "and let's see if there's a weather update. Maybe it's going to get better." As she switched on the radio David asked, "Where's Dad?"

"Gone to the city, of course. Left us here on a day like this without even a telephone and . . . what's that!"

The lights flickered briefly. The radio sputtered with static.

"Oh no!" wailed his mother. "We're going to lose the electricity!"

David tried to reassure her but a moment later the lights went out and did not come back on again. While her son scurried around the cottage searching for oil lamps or candles, Alice McHugh furiously blamed her absent husband for everything including the power failure. David had never seen her so upset.

He had to admit the weather was enough to upset anyone. When he glanced out the window it looked more like winter than summer. Although it was not yet teatime the sky was already as dark as twilight. A wind had sprung up, too, howling about the eaves of the cottage and rattling the windowpanes.

His mother grew more and more nervous. David forced himself to act calm for her sake. "It's only a summer storm, it will blow over soon," he assured her. He was frightened too, inside, but he knew he was the man in the family for now and he must act like one.

He built a fire in the small fireplace in the sitting room and his mother drew up a chair, stretching out her hands toward the heat. "Stay there and relax, Mom," he said. "Everything's okay." Going into the kitchen, David began brewing a pot of tea for the two of them on the gas hob. As he waited for the kettle to boil he felt a strange vibration in the floor. The boards seemed to be rumbling under their surface of worn lino.

Could it be an earthquake? Surely not, Ireland didn't have earthquakes, he knew. An occasional tremor, but even those were very rare.

Then what was growling beneath his very feet?

Suddenly an image flashed through his brain. He recalled standing on the bank of that ring fort with Molly, and sensing something vast and shapeless buried in the earth below. It had been asleep then. He could not say how he knew, but he knew.

Just as he knew it was awake now. Awake and growling.

"Is the tea ready yet?" his mother asked from the doorway.

David whirled around. "Do you feel that?"

"Feel what?"

He started to say, Do you feel the floor shaking, then realised it would frighten her even more. So he just shrugged. But she did not seem to feel anything unusual. She crossed the kitchen and started taking cups for their tea out of the cupboard.

When the water boiled David was sorry to turn off the cheerful little flame.

They carried their tea back into the sitting room to drink by the light of the fire. Darkness pressed against the windows from outside.

When he heard the sound of the car David jumped up so quickly he spilled his tea, but his mother didn't scold him. She was right behind him as he ran to the door.

"Arthur!" she cried. "Where have you been?"

As he got out of the car, Professor McHugh replied, "In Cork City, of course. I told you this morning I would be at the university all day."

"Well I'm glad you're back now!" said his wife, putting her arms around him and hugging hard.

Over her head, Arthur McHugh gave his son a surprised look. "What's all this about, David?"

"The storm. We had sleet here for a while. Later the power went off and I guess she got scared."

"Were *you* scared?" his father asked as the three went into the cottage together.

David shrugged manfully. "What's a little sleet?"

"Unusual, this time of year," replied Professor McHugh. "Alice, would you fix me a drink? There's some whiskey in the cupboard in the kitchen."

When she had left the room he said to his son, "It's more than a little sleet, I'm afraid. I brought the latest papers with me – look at this."

64

By the light of the fire, David read a headline: MASSIVE HAILSTONES FALL ON WATERFORD.

Professor McHugh unfolded another newspaper and held it toward him. Two words stood out in stark black letters: KILLER ICE!

It was that morning's edition of one of the national papers. Taking it from his father, David sank down on a chair by the fire to read. The city of Dublin, he learned, had awakened to find itself sheathed in ice. Cars had skidded and crashed, power lines were down, people were being asked to check on elderly neighbours.

David looked up at his father. "What's happening?"

"I don't know, no one can say for sure. The weather's gone crazy."

"You said the climate was changing."

"Yes, but surely not this fast. This is freakish – and very dangerous. It's not just car crashes and ice on the wires. Long term, this could disrupt the entire agricultural business. A lot of farmers will lose everything if the weather doesn't return to normal."

But the weather did not improve. That night David and his family ate their dinner by candlelight and went to bed to listen to the wind howling outside and sleet once again rattling the windows.

The next morning the electricity flickered briefly and the radio leaped to life in the middle of a newscast. But almost at once it went off again. David's mother moaned.

Arthur McHugh said, "I'll go out and see what's happening."

"Can I come with you?" his son asked eagerly.

"I want you to stay here, David, and take care of your mother."

As the car drove away the lights flickered again. Then they came back on and a newscaster's familiar voice issued from the radio.

"See, Mom," said David with a confidence he did not feel. "Everything's going to be all right."

"No it's not," she replied in a strained voice. "Listen to this."

The newscaster was saying, " . . . and we have just received reports of an elderly couple who were found frozen to death in their room in a Limerick B & B last night. They were believed to be tourists. No one is certain how long they had been dead, but gardai are investigating."

"Do you hear that?" cried David's mother. "Frozen to death in a bed and breakfast! So what's going to happen to us?"

"They probably had electric heat and the electricity went off, just as it did here. And you heard the radio, they were elderly; old people can't take the cold. We have a fireplace and plenty of fuel and the power's back on, we're going to be fine, Mom."

Alice McHugh's voice grew shrill. "I want to go

home. I want to go home *now*. Where's your father gone with the car? Why doesn't he come back?"

"He just left. He went into the village to try and find out what's happening, he'll be back soon."

"He better," David's mother said grimly. "I'll never forgive him for dragging us down here."

"He didn't drag us, Mom. You insisted on coming, remember? And it's just as bad in Dublin."

But Professor McHugh did not return.

CHAPTER TWELVE

As the hours dragged by, David's mother grew more and more upset. "Your father's forgotten all about us. He's gone off to one of those precious megaliths of his and left us here to fend for ourselves."

"He wouldn't do that, Mom," David said with conviction.

"Would he not? You don't know him like I do. Let me tell you . . . "

Alice McHugh began recounting to her horrified son all the grievances of her marriage. David realised she was frightened and worried, but he wished she would not say these things to him. He didn't want to know.

At last he pulled on his heaviest jumper and his jacket and announced, "I'm going over to the Doyle farm. They'll know what's happening and they have a telephone. I'll try to find out where Dad is. He might be at the university," he added lamely, though he did not really think so.

"I don't want you going out in this weather," protested his mother.

"I'll be grand. Look, the sleet's stopped and the wind has died down. I'll just run over there and come right back. You'll be all right for a little while, won't you?"

"I suppose so," she said doubtfully. She was torn between her fear of being alone and her desire to know what was happening. "But hurry back!"

"I will," David promised.

When he stepped outside the cold hit him like a fist. Frozen blades of grass crunched like crystal beneath his feet. It was no longer summer. It was the dead of winter and getting colder every minute.

He set off toward the Doyle farm.

As he crossed the fields, frozen ruts threatened to turn his ankles. The wind began to howl again and pluck at his clothes with icy fingers. Within minutes a blizzard of ice crystals was swirling around him, stinging his face and taking his breath away. Though he knew it was around noon, the day was as dark as evening.

Ice Age evening.

I'm back in my nightmare, David thought, feeling fear catch him by the throat. But he knew it wasn't a nightmare.

He began to run.

At last he saw the Doyle farmhouse ahead, with lights glowing in the windows. Their power was on too, then. Somehow the sight of those golden rectangles of light made David feel better. He scolded himself for being a baby. It was ridiculous to let a cold spell and a power failure scare him.

He trotted, breathless, to the door and banged the knocker. After a long wait he heard someone coming.

"Mol . . ." he began, but it was not Molly who opened the door.

Mr. Doyle peered out at him. "What are you doing coming out in such weather, lad?"

"Is Molly here?"

"And where else would she be?"

"We don't have a phone at the cottage, and my father went off in the car hours ago and hasn't come back. My mother's getting scared, so I thought . . ."

"Of course, of course, you want to use our phone. Come on in, lad. Molly!" Mr. Doyle raised his voice in a shout. "David's here!"

Molly emerged from the kitchen, wiping her hands on a towel. Her cheeks were pink and glowing and David was very glad to see her. She looked warm and safe and sensible. "You'll have a cup of tea," she said immediately.

"I need to make a phone call and then get back. My mother's alone."

"Of course. The phone's inside, come on."

But when David lifted the receiver all he heard was dead air.

"I'm afraid the phone isn't working," he told Mr. Doyle ruefully.

"Who did you want to ring?"

"The university, I guess. My father might be there."

"Well if he is, surely to God he'll have sense enough to stay there until the storm passes and the weather improves."

David could not help asking, "Will it improve?"

"It will of course, lad," the farmer replied. "Does it not always?" But although he spoke in a hearty tone, David thought he heard a hollow note.

Mr. Doyle was not sure either.

When Molly insisted their visitor have a cup of tea, her father and David followed her into the kitchen. Oil lamps were burning in case the lights went out again and there was a lingering smell of cooked breakfast. The comfortable room seemed like a warm golden cave. David accepted a brimming mug of tea and held it with both hands, letting the heat thaw his frozen fingers.

"You're shivering," the girl remarked.

"I know."

"Why don't you sit by the Aga and get warm, while I go over to the cottage and bring your mother back here?" Mr. Doyle suggested. "We can leave a note there for your Da."

"That would be grand, but . . . "

"But what?"

How could David explain to the kindly farmer that his mother might well refuse to go off in a car with a "strange man"? She was always mistrustful of strangers. "I'd better go with you," he said.

"Nonsense. I'm able to collect one little woman and bring her back safely. You stay here now and keep Molly company." Without listening to any further protest, Mr. Doyle was gone.

Outside the farmhouse the wind shrieked and howled. The youngsters drank tea and deliberately talked about everything but the weather. Then a silence fell. All that could be heard was the ticking of the clock on the wall – and the wailing wind.

Molly gave David a long look. "You're really scared, aren't you?"

"I am scared." It felt good to be able to admit it. "You know, there are some things we really depend on. We think they'll always be the same and be there for us. Like summer. Like our parents."

Molly said, "Everything changes, it has to. That's nature's way. If you lived on a farm you'd know that. Every season is different, no crop is like the last one. And," she added in a lower voice, "even parents die."

"Oh Molly, I'm sorry. I didn't mean to remind you . . ."

"It's all right," said the girl, though sudden tears glistened in her eyes.

Embarrassed, David went to the nearest window and looked out. For a long time he watched the scene: the scudding dark clouds, the trees whipping in the gale, the cold blue light that looked like

December instead of July. He stood without moving, but his mind was racing.

At last he turned back toward Molly. "I think I may be to blame for the climate changing," he said.

"Don't be daft!"

"I mean it. Remember when my father quoted Yeats: ' . . . our memories are part of one great memory, the memory of nature herself'?"

"I do remember. But what has that to do with the weather, David?"

"I think I've tapped into . . . into nature's memory. There's something in the earth that has never forgotten the Ice Age. It's been waiting there all this time until I touched it somehow – perhaps through the stones. Maybe the people who put them up in the first place meant them to be a kind of magic to hold back the cold. We think people in the Stone Age worshipped the sun, but perhaps they had racial memories of the Ice Age and some of the monuments they erected were meant to keep the ice from coming back."

"If they were," said Molly, "it worked. In school they taught us that Ireland has been warm for nine thousand years. I thought the Gulf Stream was responsible, though."

David nodded. "That's what they taught us too. But Ireland's getting cold again now, and fast. And I think I set it off."

"Even if you did – and I'm not saying I agree with you – what can you do about it now?"

Before he could answer, an explosion of sleet hit the window like pellets from a shotgun. David jumped back. When he turned toward Molly his face was very pale. "I don't know yet, but I have to do something. Maybe it's not too late to reverse the process."

"We don't even know what the process is."

"If I'm right," said David earnestly, "it began when I first visited that stone circle of yours. So maybe that's the place to start."

Molly looked past him toward the window. "We'd best wait until the weather improves."

"That's the point. What if it doesn't improve? If we wait it may only get worse."

"Colder, you mean?"

Suddenly David recalled his dreams in every vivid detail. How could he make her understand? "The Ice Age covered a lot of Europe at one time, Molly. And it was more than cold. It was desolate. I've had nightmares . . . nothing was alive. Nothing. There was only the ice and the wind. It was worse than being dead, it was like never having been.

"If it covers Ireland again, everything here will die. The grass, the plants, the animals. We'll all have to leave – unless it expands to cover the earth. Then where would we go?"

Molly's blue eyes were enormous. "Could that really happen?"

"I don't know. A few days ago I would have said this weather couldn't really happen."

"And you think you might be able to do something about it? Should you not wait for my father to get back with your mother?"

"How long has he been gone?"

Molly glanced at the clock on the mantle. "Why . . . it's been an hour."

"It doesn't take an hour to drive from here to our place," David said grimly. "Something's happened to them. And something's happened to my father, too."

"I'm scared, David," she said in a harsh whisper.

"I'm scared too." The boy reached for his jacket. "But I'm not going to just wait here and let it happen."

CHAPTER THIRTEEN

As soon as he decided to do something, David felt better. He was no less afraid, but he did not feel so much like a victim. If his parents had been with him he would not have felt he must do this himself; grownups were supposed to take care of things.

But the grownups had gone.

The look Molly gave him was part concern and part admiration. "If you're going out there, I'm going too," she said.

"You are not. I won't let you."

"And how are you going to stop me?" She put her hands on her hips and stared at him defiantly. "Besides, I don't want to be left here by myself."

After a moment's hesitation, David said, "Okay, come on then. But put on all the warm clothes you have."

She soon returned with an armload of sweaters and scarves. "These are my Da's. You need more warm clothes too."

When the youngsters were heavily wrapped in layers of clothing, Molly looked at David and burst into laughter. "You're fat!"

"So are you," he told her. "And we'll need every layer."

He took one last look around the warm room. How easy it would be just to stay there. Surely the wind would die down, the storm would blow over, their parents would come back . . .

No. David shook his head. Somehow he knew that was not going to happen. Not unless he made it happen.

His father had said he had a gift. But it was a curse. And he was the only one who could lift it.

When they opened the door the wind screamed at them and almost tore the door out of their hands. David ducked his chin deep into his collar. "Are you sure?" he asked Molly, giving her one last chance to back out.

She nodded. "Let's go."

Wind buffeted them from all sides. When David tried to turn his back to it, he found it was blowing in his face as well. He had never known a wind to do that before.

It sucked the moisture out of his lungs and made them burn. He wrapped a scarf around the lower part of his face and breathed through the fabric. Molly imitated him, covering her nose and mouth with a swathe of blue wool that was almost the colour of her eyes.

Heads down, the pair of them trudged off across the field. Sleet pelted them. Then the particles of sleet became larger, became hail that drummed on their heads like rocks, making them gasp and flinch. They seemed to walk for hours. Most of the time David kept his chin down and his eyes on the ground, occasionally glancing up to see if they were there yet. Whenever he raised his face the slashing wind brought tears to his eyes.

At last he saw the stone circle ahead of them. The stones looked . . . darker than he remembered, though perhaps that was because the afternoon itself was so dark. An awful thought struck David. What time was it? Would night fall soon and catch them out here?

Molly took hold of his arm. "What are you going to do now?"

He did not answer. As they walked he had been trying to make some sort of plan, but faced with the forbidding reality of the circle, his plan seemed silly. He felt very small and young . . . and helpless.

"Where did it begin, exactly?" asked Molly, shouting over the wind.

"Over there." He pointed. "Between those pillar stones."

"Then that's where we start." She started toward the stones.

The boy hastily trotted after her. "Don't, Molly. I think I have to do this by myself. But . . . stay close, will you? Where I can see you?"

"I'll stand right here," she promised. "But if anything goes wrong, I'm coming for you." There was a determined jut to her wool-swathed jaw that told him she meant every word.

Step by step, David approached the pillar stones. He did not think he could feel any colder than he was, but all of a sudden his body seemed to turn to a block of solid ice.

He glanced back. Molly nodded to him encouragingly.

Another step, and then another.

The world spun around him and he heard again the ringing in his ears. His stomach lurched in anticipation. *Concentrate,* he told himself. Think of warm things. Think of green grass and summer sun. Think of bread baking in an Aga. Think of life.

Another step, and then another.

The wind howled in rage. Pellets of ice scored his cheeks. One cut so deeply a tiny trickle of blood seeped out, but froze on his skin.

He reached the pillar stones. In spite of the howling of the wind he could hear a sound coming from them, a low, angry buzzing.

They knew he was there.

The darkness of the afternoon seemed to gather itself into one gigantic ball of night that settled in the stone circle just beyond the pillar stones. At first it had no shape. But as David watched, it assumed roughly circular dimensions and became the vast being he had glimpsed . . . sensed . . . beneath the ground at the ring fort.

It was a monster but it was not alive. It had never been alive. It was the enemy of all life: the dark, the cold, the spirit of the ice.

It had lain in the earth for nine thousand years or more. Once this entire land had been its domain. An island kingdom sheathed in ice.

It knew he was there. The warm thing. When the sun flared and grew hotter, driving it underground, the warm things had flooded into its kingdom. It could sense them scurrying over the earth like so many insects. Buried deep in the ground, it envied them their life and freedom of movement.

The spirit of the ice had never left the island. Anything with that much power could not die. It could only wait. It had waited in the Irish earth as others like itself waited in other parts of the world, anticipating when their time would come round again.

As eons passed, its dim, cold thoughts had reached the surface and touched the tiny minds of the warm ones. They had felt an instinctive fear. None of them remembered the Ice Age. But their prehistoric ancestors had crouched in caves thousands of years earlier and stared out in horror at the advancing glaciers as they relentlessly spread south from the Pole.

The people in the caves had fled from the ice, seeking warmer lands. When after thousands of years the glaciers melted, some of their descendants had made their way to Ireland in frail leather boats. They found a green island with a mild climate and made it their home.

Those Stone Age settlers had been unaware of what lay beneath the surface.

Until the spirit of the ice became aware of them.

For a time it had been content to wait. Then, growing restless, it reached out and touched their minds. It filled their dreams with images of itself.

In terror they turned to magic for protection. They erected sacred stones to stand guard over caves and fissures which they believed were entrances to the underground world. But still they were aware of the spirit of the ice, lurking. Compared to its strength, theirs was nothing.

The Stone Age people realised that the cold had one powerful enemy, however. So they built other stones into monuments to court the sun. Every winter they pleaded with the sun to return and not leave them to become victims of the monster under the ground.

The spirit of the ice remembered.

Time passed on the surface. The thing in the earth cared nothing for time. It could not age or die.

The warm ones gave way to other warm ones with different customs, but they too felt an instinctive fear of something that lurked underground. They responded by burying offerings deep in the soil near ancient holy places. The ice spirit had accepted their homage with indifference. They had nothing it wanted – except the land itself.

CHAPTER FOURTEEN

No matter how much change took place on the surface, the spirit of the ice remained unaffected below. It was not disturbed by man's so-called progress or his petty wars. The things human beings did were no more to it than the buzzing of gnats to a mountain.

Then after long ages, a touch from the surface reached deep into the earth. Briefly, shockingly, one of the gnats had made contact with the slumbering giant.

Like needles thrust into its hide, the stones had carried the message. And slowly, ponderously, the spirit in the earth awakened.

One of the warm ones was reaching out to it

The spirit of the ice could not think, as humans think. But it could respond to energy. The boy's energy had called and it had replied. A link was forged between them. A link between the cold darkness in which it lay, and the surface land it had once possessed. Along that slender chain the force that had once dominated the land began to return.

The time of waiting was almost over.

David paused between the two pillar stones. A shock ran through his body. The sound the stones made was becoming a loud hum. If he put his hand on one, it would vibrate beneath his touch.

He wanted to look back at Molly for reassurance, but he knew he had to concentrate. When the . . . whatever it was . . . had gripped him before, he had broken free by thinking. He had summoned images of everything warm and bright and living and clung to them. He must do that again. He must somehow *will* the cold away.

In his mind he pictured Dublin in the summer, with the trees in full leaf and blackbirds in the garden. He imagined the sun beaming down on the street where he lived, heating the pavement. Reflecting from the windows of the houses. Sun on the sand of the beaches, sun dazzling the windscreens of cars.

Hot, bright . . . David thought of Mrs. Quinlan's flower garden next door, vivid with bright red roses and yellow sunflowers, glowing in the sunshine!

The wind screamed at him. The cold threatened to suffocate him.

He thought of the Doyles' kitchen with the Aga radiating heat. And a mug of hot tea in his hands. And a fire blazing in the sitting room, and warm blankets, and scalding hot baths. And sunshine outside, banishing the clouds and the ice. Always the brilliant sun . . .

The cold seemed to lessen just a little.

With a terrific effort of will, David expanded his mental imagery. He pictured a map of Ireland and tried to think of himself as a bird, with the island spread out below him. See it a lush and brilliant green, see it bathed in hot yellow sunlight from coast to coast!

"David! Are you all right?"

Molly's voice was coming to him from miles and miles away but he must not answer. If he answered he might lose the picture in his mind.

The thing in the earth felt the stab of a tiny pinprick of hot yellow light. It roared in fury at this touch of the ancient enemy.

On either side of David, the two pillar stones rocked violently.

"David!" screamed Molly, afraid one of them might fall on him. "Mind yourself!" But he did not seem to hear her.

She wondered if she should go to him. He was standing very still with his back to her. He looked a lonely and pathetic figure in the middle of the storm. How could one teenage boy match himself against the elements?

Yet he was trying; he was being brave and she wanted to help. She started toward him.

Something rumbled under her feet.

Molly stopped abruptly. Was the ground moving? Could it be an earthquake? She gasped as it happened again and a great crack opened in the earth, running almost from her feet to the pillar stones where David stood. From the crack a white mist rose like a cloud of frost. The wind caught it and swirled it into wild patterns.

In spite of her fear, Molly recognised one of those patterns. She had seen the same design on the gold circlet David had discovered near the dolmen.

A low, angry roar was coming from the opening in the earth. It grew and grew until it became a mighty bellow of thunder that echoed back from the massed clouds above. The crack in the ground yawned wider.

Looking toward David, Molly discovered he was standing on the very brink of a gaping abyss. Another moment and he would topple in.

She flung herself forward and struck him with all her might, knocking him sideways.

The two youngsters ricocheted into one of the standing stones. It swayed for a moment, then fell with a crash.

The earth opened even wider to receive it, then closed again with a sound of rock being crushed by tremendous forces.

The wind slowly died. The afternoon grew very still.

Panting, Molly and David stared at one another.

"What happened?" he said at last.

"There was this big crack in the ground. You were about to fall in it so I knocked you to one side." She pointed to the earth, where a great zigzag scar of bare soil cut through the frosted grass.

But even as they looked the frost began to melt.

The clouds parted. A tentative ray of sunshine peeped through to illumine the single large boulder that stood off to one side by itself.

"Look, David! You did it, the storm's over!" Molly clapped her hands together in excitement.

"Did I?" He sounded numb. He felt numb. There were areas in his brain that felt bruised – and cold; terribly cold.

CHAPTER FIFTEEN

With Molly at his side, David made his way back across the field to the Doyles' farmhouse. Sometimes he stumbled, but Molly held his arm and would not let him fall. He had never been so tired in his life. In some strange way he could *feel* the stone circle behind him, but he never looked back.

"Are you all right?" Molly asked him several times. He no longer minded having anyone ask. He was just thankful to be with somebody who cared. "I'm tired and I have a headache, but I'm okay," he told her.

She did not like the way he looked, however. The boy's eyes were sunken in his head and ringed with dark circles. His face was sickly white and he staggered like an old man.

But the weather was definitely improving.

By the time the two had made their way across the long, mucky field that lay between the stone circle and the farmyard, the wind had fallen dramatically. There was no sleet, merely a drizzle of soft rain. Then even that stopped.

The sky grew lighter. A hint of sun peeped through the clouds.

Molly gave a shaky but relieved laugh. "Irish weather!" she said. "Look, David!"

But David was looking at something else. Parked in front of the farmhouse was Liam Doyle's battered old car – and behind it, Arthur McHugh's!

With a shout, David broke into a run.

The three adults were gathered in the Doyles' sitting room, bundled in coats and looking as if they were about to go outside. When David burst into the room with Molly close behind him, he saw relief on all their faces.

"We were going to go searching for you, son," said Professor McHugh.

Molly's father added, "When we got back here and you were both gone we were worried. That terrible storm . . . but it's over now."

David nodded. "It is over . . . for now," he said.

Later, as they sat in front of the fireplace and Molly served tea to everyone, David pieced together the day's events. His father had gone as far as the nearest village, all right, but there he had car trouble. The local mechanic told him he should have had anti-freeze in his car. "In the summer!" Arthur McHugh exclaimed indignantly.

They were still trying to get the car running

some hours later. By the time it was finally back on the road, Liam Doyle had arrived at the cottage to collect Mrs. McHugh. But as David had expected, she was reluctant to come away with him. He was trying to persuade her when her husband came driving down the lane.

After brief explanations all around, the trio intended to go to the farm. "We were going to bring you back home," Alice McHugh told her son. "But we only got as far as our own gate when the storm got so bad we couldn't drive. I've never seen anything like it."

Her husband agreed. "Wind and hail and darkness all together. Even an awful roaring thunder. For a while I thought the storm was strong enough to turn our cars over."

"It could have done," declared Liam Doyle. "We just sat where we were and waited it out, that's all we could do. There should never have been thunder," he added, shaking his head. "A freak storm, that's what it was. A real freak."

Alice McHugh said, "David, whatever possessed the two of you to go off in such weather? Why did you not wait here in the house where you were safe?"

"Safe?" David and Molly exchanged glances. "We didn't feel very safe," the girl replied cautiously. She was not sure how much David would want to tell his parents.

"We went looking for help," said the boy. He did

not explain where they looked or what help they sought. Sitting in front of the blazing fire with people all around him, the events in the stone circle seemed remote, dreamlike. He did not think he could make anyone else understand.

Except Molly. Molly had been there.

Her blue eyes met his. "Well, the storm's over now," she said. "That's the important thing."

Mrs. McHugh nodded. "It is indeed, and we've all had a hard day. Arthur, I think we should go home this minute and go to bed. I imagine the Doyles would like to do the same."

No one disagreed.

As they drove back to the cottage, for once David's parents were not having a row. They seemed at peace with one another.

He hoped they would stay that way.

But when he finally snuggled beneath the duvet and all the blankets he could pile on his bed, he could not sleep. He kept waiting to hear the sounds of the storm again.

Deep in the bruised places in his brain he knew it was not over.

CHAPTER SIXTEEN

In the morning the sun was shining when David woke up. He lay in bed for a few minutes, letting the world come into focus around him. He found himself listening for sounds that would reassure him the world had returned to normal. When a bird trilled beyond his window, he grinned and jumped out of bed.

Maybe I'm wrong, he told himself. Maybe everything will be all right now.

All through breakfast he tried to hold on to that thought. But though the day began well, his parents had another row while they were still sitting at the breakfast table. This time it was over a matter as unimportant as the toast.

Arthur McHugh said it was burnt, his wife said it was perfect and he was just being picky.

"I'm not picky."

"Hyper-critical then. Do you like it better when I use big words? Do you want me to sound like one of those giddy students who flutter their eyelashes at you? Then maybe you'd pay some attention to me, instead of . . ."

"Be quiet, Alice," David's father said in a low voice, casting a meaningful glance at his son. "This isn't the time or the place."

Her voice rose. "There's never a good time or place, is there? You just don't want to face this."

Her husband pushed his chair back from the table. "I have to meet Charlie Ryan," he announced.

"This is the first I've heard. You don't have to meet anyone, you're just running away from the issue the way you always do. An Irish solution for an Irish problem . . ."

David didn't wait to hear anymore. Blotting his mouth with his napkin, he excused himself and left the kitchen even ahead of his father.

He went to the front door and opened it to gaze out at the day. The sky overhead was a radiant blue, and the sun to the east dazzled his eyes.

He thought of going over to see Molly, but somehow he did not want to be with anyone, even her. Those bruised places were still in his brain. And deep in his body was a coldness the sunlight did not touch.

Although the day seemed warm enough, he shrugged into a lightweight denim jacket. Then he left the cottage and set off along the laneway to the road beyond. He had no clear idea where he was going.

His father's car soon caught up with him. Braking, Arthur McHugh rolled down his window. "I'm on my way in to the city, son. Want to come along?"

David shook his head. "If you have an appointment with Professor Ryan you don't need me there."

"I . . . I don't have an appointment," his father admitted. "I just . . . well, you know how it is."

"Sure." The boy's shoulders slumped. "I know how it is."

"So do you want to come with me? We could look at some of the artefacts they have in the university collection."

"I don't think so, Dad. But thanks anyway."

His father gave him a long look. "Suit yourself, then." He rolled up the window and drove away a little too fast.

I've hurt his feelings, David thought when it was too late. I should have gone with him.

But he did not want to be with his father any more than he wanted to be with Molly. Or even less; he certainly did not want to look at ancient artefacts. The sight of one might close the connection again.

He trudged along the road with his head down and his hands deep in his pockets. But as he walked, he gradually began to feel better. The birds were singing; the sun was shining. And when he began to look around he recognised some of the flowers Molly had pointed out to him. Their bright faces gazed back at him from the hedgerows, assuring him everything was as it should be. Ireland in the summer. Crazy weather, maybe, but Irish weather had a reputation for being crazy.

He was daft, he told himself. Worse than daft; he was conceited to think he, David McHugh, had anything at all to do with the weather, or any power to change it. What had happened yesterday was the wildest coincidence, nothing more.

"You have a great imagination," his teachers were always telling him. And so he did – this was the proof. He had invented a whole fantasy in his head and Molly had played along with him. He should be ashamed. He was fifteen years old! Yet like a stupid little kid he had scared himself for nothing.

For nothing.

His eye fell to the verge of the road, where a car had driven onto the soft shoulder. In the deeply rutted mud ice crystals still glinted.

David stared down at the ice.

He did not tell his body to crouch down beside the ruts, but it did. He did not tell his fingers to reach out and touch the tiny frozen crystals, but they did.

When he lifted his hand, a few of the crystals clung to the warm skin of his fingertips. Hesitantly, he touched them to his tongue.

At first it just tasted like . . . nothing. Like ice. But

then his mouth filled with the flavour of the sea. Iodine. Salt. And something incredibly bitter, like sour soil that has not seen sunlight for a million years.

David wiped his fingers on his jacket. But the taste remained in his mouth.

Why did I do that? he asked himself angrily.

He stood up and strode away.

On his tongue lay the flavour of ancient time.

As he walked, the lush summer landscape of Cork seemed to shimmer faintly around him. He stopped. He made himself look – hard – at the nearest hedgerow. Everything seemed normal. But when he began to walk on, the landscape shimmered again.

He turned around and headed back toward the cottage. At least, he meant to go back toward the cottage. But when he looked down the road the way he had just come, nothing seemed familiar.

David broke into a trot. The farther he went, the more convinced he became that he was lost. Inside his jacket he began to sweat. At the same time the coldness inside him seemed to expand, filling him up.

When he saw a pathway that looked vaguely familiar he turned onto it and followed its winding course for several minutes. Then his way was blocked by overgrown bramble hedges. He turned around to go back, only to notice another pathway off to one side.

David stopped to glance at the sky. Yes, this second path ran east, toward the morning sun. Surely the cottage lay to the east.

He set off again. After a few more minutes he came to a Y where the path branched off in two directions. When he glanced skyward to see which way was east, he realised the sun had gone.

The sky was filled with clouds.

And under his feet, a low rumble began.

CHAPTER SEVENTEEN

David was thoroughly frightened now. He whirled around to go back the way he had come, only to discover to his horror that the brambles had closed the path. He must take one fork of the Y. No other way was open to him.

Whatever was growling in the earth was drawing closer. The vibrations came up through the ground and into his bones.

He stared wildly around, trying to think what to do. The day had grown very still – aside from the ominous noise underground. Not a leaf stirred. No bird sang. The whole world seemed to be holding its breath.

Beneath the gathering clouds the light changed; became flat and silvery.

He could not just stand there and wait for . . . for whatever it was. David decided on the left fork of the path and hurried forward.

Having made a decision, even if there was no

particular reason for his choice, calmed the pounding of his heart a little. He wasn't helpless; he was doing something.

As he followed the path it seemed increasingly familiar in some way he could not name. He had never been in this exact place before, yet it was set in a landscape he knew, he felt sure. If only he could see over the brambles that crowded close on either side!

Then all at once the brambles gave way and he found himself standing on a hillside at the head of a valley.

Just below him was the stone circle.

Alone in the cottage, Alice McHugh busied herself for a time doing the washing up and making the beds. Then she got out the cranky old hoover that came with the house and gave everything a cleaning. But the cottage was small and all too soon her work was done. Going into the bathroom, she opened the hamper to see how much dirty laundry had accumulated. There was no washing machine, of course. Leave it to Arthur to take a house with no washing machine! Most things must wait to go to the launderette in the nearest town. But meanwhile there was some hand wash to do; she did her underthings by hand, and liked to hang them outside to dry so they would smell fresh.

She was just pinning the last item to the

clothesline by the back door of the cottage when the first snowflakes fell.

At the Doyle farm, Liam Doyle and two hired men were moving livestock from one pasture to another. Molly was alone in the house but she did not mind being alone. She was in her room, trying out new ways to plait her hair in front of the mirror. When she had it done to suit her she meant to get on her bike and go over to David's.

She found herself leaning closer to the mirror than usual. It was hard to see what she was doing. Then she realised the room had got very dark.

Getting up, she went to the window and peered out.

The sky was thick with clouds.

"Another storm," she said in disgust. She switched on the electric light, then turned it off and went down the hall to the kitchen instead. In case the power failed again she wanted to be certain the Aga had plenty of fuel. Her father and the men would want their tea when they came back, electricity or no.

The girl checked the Aga, then went to the kitchen door and looked out.

Her mouth fell open in astonishment.

Great flakes of snow were drifting out of the sky.

The cold David had been carrying around inside him all day now surrounded him. He began shivering; he zipped up his jacket but that did not help. A bitter wind had begun to blow across the valley.

But at least he knew where he was now, that was something. If he had come out close to the stone circle, then only a stretch of muddy field stood between him and the Doyles' farmhouse. Relieved, he started forward.

Then he stopped.

Try as he might, when he looked down the valley he could not see the farmhouse. Or the barn or any outbuildings.

And was the circle itself different?

He narrowed his eyes, squinting.

The configuration he remembered was still there, but now all the stones appeared to be standing upright.

He became aware of a taste in his mouth: an almost metallic taste of iodine and ancient, sour earth.

To reach the Doyle farm – if the Doyle farm was still there – David would have to walk past the circle. Beyond the farm was the road that would lead him eventually to the cottage.

If the cottage was still there.

Don't be silly! David scolded himself. Of course it's there. You're just scaring yourself again with that wild imagination of yours.

But the rising shriek of the wind was not his imagination, nor was the rumbling beneath his feet that was growing louder all the time. And surely he was not imagining the cold. Imagination alone couldn't make his teeth chatter. The cold was terribly real.

Step by reluctant step, David advanced toward the stones.

If there were any other way to go he would have taken it. But when he turned and looked back, the path behind him had closed up completely. Only a solid wall of brambles remained, clawing the sky like menacing fingers.

He had to go on.

As he drew nearer he could see very clearly that all the stones were indeed standing upright. And they did not look so worn. Their edges were sharp as if freshly hewn. In the flat grey light they looked very black.

Beyond the circle he could see the solitary stone he had photographed the day he and his father first visited the circle. Reassuringly, it was not standing erect but lay horizontal on the ground, just as always. If he could only reach that stone . . .

David started to run.

At that moment a mighty gust of wind hit him. He staggered sideways and almost lost his balance. A small animal skittered through the grass close to his feet. He glanced toward it, expecting to see a hare or a field mouse. Instead he saw a strangely humped, furry shape he did not recognise at all, a creature from another time.

It paused momentarily as if aware of him, then raced on in panic.

David almost screamed aloud.

A snowflake drifted lazily down to alight on his sleeve. He saw its shape clearly before it melted.

The ground was shaking now. He was afraid it would open up as it had done before and swallow him. But where was safe? If he could only make it to the single stone . . .

He was very close to the circle. How sharp and new the upright stones looked, as if they had been set in place only yesterday!

And there was a sound . . . chanting . . .

David stopped and rubbed his eyes. Dim shapes were becoming visible through a swirling, snowy mist.

CHAPTER EIGHTEEN

In the Doyle farmhouse, Molly was listening apprehensively to a rising wind. Whatever had gone wrong with the weather, there was snow now in July.

After her experience with David the preceding day she did not accept the unseasonable weather as a mere freak of nature. She was not totally convinced that David was responsible, but she was certain he was mixed up in it somehow.

Her bicycle was leaning against the side of the house. Molly gave it a speculative look, then went to her room for a coat. She would ride over to the cottage before the weather got any worse and just see if David was okay.

She scribbled a note for her father in case he got back before she returned, and left it under the milk jug beside the tea things.

When she got on her bike the wind was not too bad. Keeping her head down, she pedalled down the farm lane toward the main road. But when she reached the road she stopped and stood beside her bike for a moment, undecided.

She could not say how she knew, but suddenly she was absolutely convinced David was not at the cottage. It did not *feel* as if he were at the cottage.

Molly had never had such a feeling about anyone before and she found it disturbing. How could she know where David was – or wasn't?

Well he must be someplace, she told herself, but there's no point in my standing out here on the road in a snowstorm trying to guess where he is. She ran her bike a few steps forward then jumped on and began pedalling back toward the farmhouse.

With a hungry howl, the wind slammed into the side of her bike.

Molly tried desperately to keep her balance but her strength was nothing against the force of the gale. The bicycle wobbled wildly, then fell over, throwing her into the ditch beside the laneway. Her head struck a stone and the darkness closed in on her.

The voice of the wind beyond the cottage had risen from a wail to a scream. Alice McHugh had not experienced much snow in her life, but she did not think it came with such a terrible wind. Snow was usually silent and soft, a gentle drifting.

Wasn't it?

The moment she saw the first flakes, she had been so upset she ran back into the cottage and slammed the door. All the terrors of the day before had come back to haunt her. The power would go out again, she would be left alone in the dark . . . now she stood in the middle of the living room, hugging herself and listening anxiously to the wind. A resolution was slowly forming in her mind.

"I'm tired of being left alone," she said aloud to the silent room. "I'm tired of waiting for him to come to his senses. This isn't the Dark Ages, I have rights too."

As she began to grow angry her fear diminished.

She paced from room to room of the cottage, looking out various windows to gauge the intensity of the storm. "It's a blizzard," she announced aloud. "He's left me in a blizzard this time." At least it was snow rather than ice. The roads would not be as dangerous, and perhaps the lights would stay on.

She wanted her husband to come back, and the sooner the better. They had a lot to discuss. They could not keep papering over the cracks of their marriage and pretending everything was going to be all right.

There was David to consider, too. Children were so conservative. They resisted any sort of change, and David more than most. But his parents' relationship had been decaying for a long time.

Perhaps he would not even be too surprised. He was an intelligent boy, and in some ways he was mature for his age. Eventually he would understand that his parents simply could not spend the rest of their lives together. Neither of them had wanted their marriage to break down, but change was a part of life. Like the weather.

Like the weather, Alice McHugh thought with a bitter smile.

Arthur McHugh was nearing Cork City when the first snowflakes appeared like tiny stars on his windscreen. When he glanced in the rear view mirror he saw that the western sky was appallingly dark. He took his foot off the accelerator and let the car coast for fifty yards or so. Should he turn around and go back? Alice would tear strips off him for leaving her to face another storm so soon.

But she was a grown woman, after all. He knew that deep down she was strong and resourceful, no matter how much she enjoyed playing the helpless female. A lot of that was for David's benefit. If he wasn't careful, she would make a mama's boy out of the lad.

No, he told himself, that was not fair. Alice, whatever her other faults, was a good mother. Perhaps without him to lean on so heavily she would become more of a person in her own right.

With a start, he realised he was admitting for the first time that their marriage was all but over.

The car was still coasting. Guiltily, he stepped on the pedal again and speeded up.

What about David? Arthur McHugh thought as he drove on. How would the boy take it? He had been acting strange lately, ever since they came to Cork. His experiences with the stones and the artefacts had shaken the lad, perhaps even opened up a new world for him. One day he might . . .

A gust of wind hit the car with such force it rocked.

Snatched out of his musings, Arthur McHugh looked in the rear view mirror again. The sky was even darker and, incredibly, jagged streaks of lightning were tearing through the clouds although snow continued to fall.

This time he did not hesitate. Watching for the nearest lay-by, he turned the car around as soon as he could and headed back.

When Liam Doyle returned to the farmhouse he stuck his head in through the kitchen door, feeling the outrush of warmth on his numbed face. The blizzard had caught them as they were returning from the farthest pasture and he and his helpers were chilled to the bone. He called out, "Molly girl! Where are you?"

Silence answered him.

He glanced over his shoulder at the two men standing with their shoulders hunched against the storm. "Och, she's in her room, she'll be down in a minute," he told them. "Come in lads and have a wee drop of something. Good job we finished when we did."

But when he stepped into the kitchen, the first thing he noticed was Molly's note with one end under the milk jug. As he read, a deep frown creased his forehead. "Gone over to David's? In this weather – after yesterday? The girl is daft. Those two youngsters . . . "

He shook his head. "I'll not go running around again, the lassie can stay where she is until this blows over."

CHAPTER NINETEEN

Molly felt sick to her stomach and her head hurt. Her head hurt a lot.

And she was so very cold!

Groaning, she struggled to sit up. At first she neither knew nor cared where she was. She felt so awful that nothing else mattered.

David.

David needs me.

She did not know how she knew, but she knew. With that realisation the world swam into focus. She was in a ditch beside the laneway, and already a drift of snow half-covered her.

Snow. David.

Getting to her feet seemed to take forever. The slightest movement made her dizzy and nauseous, but she knew she could not stay in the ditch and die. She had to help herself.

And David.

Where was he?

She stood swaying on her feet, trying to recapture that sense of David she had experienced before when she *knew* he was not at the cottage. Like a dowser, she thought. I must dowse for David.

The wind swirled around her, laden with snow as thick as a cloud of white goose-down. In the ditch, her red bicycle lay on its side like a wounded animal. There was no point in getting it out right now, she decided. A bicycle would be of no use where she was going.

The cold served one useful purpose. The air was so crisp and sharp it cut through the nausea and made her stomach feel better, though the effort of walking made her head feel worse. When she reached up, she could feel a bump rising on the side of her head above the ear. The slightest touch from her fingers made her want to vomit again.

It could be bad, she knew with a country girl's experience. Fractured skull, possibly?

But she kept walking. She did not have any choice. The way she felt she could only sustain one thought at a time, and right now that thought was for David.

David needs me.

Within the newly-erected stone circle, people were chanting. Soon David could pick out individual voices: a woman's clear tones, a man's resonant bass. He crept closer. He still could not see clearly

111

as the blizzard billowed around him, but he took comfort in knowing he was not alone.

When he reached the pillar stones at the entrance, he stopped. Though the ground still shook beneath his feet, it seemed more of a sustained vibration than a quake that could split the earth open.

Now he could see them. Perhaps two dozen people were inside the stone circle. They were marching solemnly in an anti-clockwise direction, and as they passed each stone they bowed.

There was no blizzard within the circle.

David stared. No snow, no ice! Within that round space the sun shone!

For some reason that frightened him more than anything he had seen. All the laws of nature were suspended. Anything might happen now.

At his back he could still feel the cold, the terrible, killing cold. Yet nothing on earth could have forced him to step inside the circle.

He could feel the thing which lay beneath the earth, under the circle. It was accepting the reverence of those who marched and chanted, but it did not care about them. It lay in eternal night and vast, cosmic indifference.

No. Not indifference. With a thrill of horror, David realised it was aware of his presence.

The vibration in the earth changed pitch.

As he watched, the stone circle and the people within it began to fade. In another moment they were gone. He was facing an expanse of glacial whiteness.

The cold of the blizzard was as nothing compared to the cold of the glacier. Once again he felt it suck the warmth and life from his lungs and knew he had very little time left.

David frantically tried to concentrate on warm images. He closed his eyes to shut out the vision of white and imagined the red and gold of a blazing fire.

The wind tore at his eyelids with icy fingers, trying to force them open. He fought back but it was too strong. When he raised his eyelids they felt heavy because his lashes were beaded with ice.

Ice was everywhere, ice was the world. And no Molly, no living blue eyes to defy all that glaring, brilliant whiteness.

David was truly alone. In that moment he almost gave up.

What difference would it make? He was so terribly cold, so unbearably tired. If he could lie down for just a little while . . . curl up with his head pillowed on his arm and fall asleep for a few minutes . . .

"David!"

The voice came from very far away. It was too much trouble to answer, too much trouble even to listen.

His knees started to buckle.

"DAVID!"

113

He did not believe it was Molly. Molly could not find him here. She lived in another, warmer age ten thousand years in the future. He would be less than dust by the time Molly Doyle was born.

So how could she be calling his name?

He staggered a few steps in the direction he thought the call came from, then stopped, listened, went off in another direction. Nothing. No one. His numbed brain tried to think but the wind hammered at his head, making thinking impossible.

When David slumped in hopelessness, his back grazed some hard surface. He turned around but there was nothing to see, nothing behind him at all. Yet he could feel something very solid. He ran a hand over the invisible object. It was . . . yes! It was the horizontal stone that lay apart from the circle. His fingers recognised the symbols cut into its surface. The carved stone did not belong in the Ice Age, yet it was here – almost.

And Molly was here too, calling him!

With the greatest effort of his life he turned his head and answered her. He thought the shout would tear his throat open, but he shouted anyway. "Molly! Over here!"

The girl gave a great sob of relief. "Where are you?"

"Here, this way!"

She tried to follow the sound of his voice. By now it was almost impossible to see anything in the blinding swirl of snow. Raising her arm to shield her face, Molly picked her way across the frozen field. Drifts of snow were piling ever deeper. The grazing's ruined, Molly thought abstractedly. We'll have to buy feed for the cows.

The nearer she got to David, the colder the day became. She was too cold by now to feel sick, or even to take notice of the throbbing in her head. The entire world seemed to have narrowed down to herself and David and snow.

Once she stumbled over a frozen clod and fell hard to her knees. She crouched there, trying to gather herself.

"Molly!"

She dragged herself to her feet and went on.

David's voice had sounded a little closer.

After twenty or thirty yards she stopped again and cupped her eyes with her hands, trying to peer through the storm and catch sight of him. At first there were only the snowflakes. Then they formed into a solid mass of white and she realised she was not looking at snow at all, but at a vast sheet of ice.

White ice.

With David standing on it. He appeared to be leaning against something, but there was nothing to lean on but the wind.

CHAPTER TWENTY

Molly broke into a shambling run. The glare from the ice was so intense David could not see her until she was very close to him, simply because he could not keep his eyes open for more than a few moments at a time. But he heard her footfalls on the glacier surface and tried to make his numbed facial muscles smile.

"I thought I'd never find you!" the girl cried as she staggered up to him. She threw both arms around him – then gasped.

He *was* leaning against something. She could feel it behind him. But there was nothing there. With a pounding heart she peered past him to be sure.

Nothing. Just the field of ice. Yet her fingers were touching stone.

"What is this, David? Where are we?"

"In the Ice Age, I think. On a glacier, maybe."

"But what's this behind you?"

How could he explain it to her when he did not

understand himself? "It's one of the stones, the one that was outside the circle."

"But I can't see it!"

"Neither can I. I can't see our own world, either – at least, our own time. But if this stone is here our time must be here too, somehow. We have to get back to it."

"Is this what happened to you before?"

"Sort of," David replied.

Molly was fighting back panic. "I don't want to be here, David!"

"Neither do I," the boy assured her.

"You got away before, can you do it again?"

"I don't know. Last time you were . . . like somebody standing on shore when I was drowning, throwing me a life jacket. This time you're with me. And there isn't anyone else to help us."

Molly swallowed hard. "Okay. Okay, I guess we have to do it for ourselves. What's the first step?"

The determination in the girl's voice steadied him. "Well, we have to imagine warm things. Heat, sun, fire."

"Is that all?"

"No, but it's a beginning. Hold the heat in your mind. Block out everything else and try to believe you're as hot as you can possibly be. Use the heat to fight against the ice. Maybe one is no more real than the other, I don't know. But do it, Molly. Do it!"

She screwed up her eyes and tried to picture

herself on a desert island; a favourite fantasy. Sand and blue sea and palm trees, and herself lying on a blanket with the sun beaming down.

But she was cold. She was so agonisingly *cold*. "I can't," she told David between clenched teeth.

"You have to. I don't know anything else to do." He caught her hand and held it with his own, but by now she could not feel his touch. Her fingers were like chips of ice. "Please, Molly. Try again."

The monster in the earth roared. Travelling up through layers of ice, its voice shook the world. Molly was so frightened she screamed back at it, "Fire and fire and fire!"

David added his voice to hers. "Fire!" they cried in unison. Then with a sudden inspiration the boy turned it into a chant: "Fire and sun, fire and sun, fire and sun!"

Against his back David felt the invisible stone growing warm, as if heat were being carried from his body down into the earth. "Molly! Put your hands on this and keep chanting!"

He guided her hands to the stone. The boy and girl pressed against it, leaning on nothing, chanting.

Slowly the wind dropped. The air was still bitterly cold, but without the wind buffeting them David felt better. "It's working, Molly. Keep on," he urged.

"But I don't know what we're doing."

"I think we're sending a message to . . . to the Ice Age," he said, though he knew that would sound crazy. "We're making it *warm*, we're making it *hot*, we're sending it fire, fire, *fire*!" he chanted.

But crazy or not, Molly trusted him. She echoed the chant. As she stood with her eyes screwed shut and her hands pressed against the invisible stone, a warm tingle ran through her body and down along her arms, into the solid rock. It came from a place inside her head where there was fire and sun and light and heat and comfort . . .

She chanted. David chanted. Time had no meaning. They would never know how long they stood there, trying to ignore the cold that gripped them.

David's arms began to get tired from tension. When he felt them starting to tremble he was momentarily distracted, and in that instant the wind began to howl again.

"Concentrate!" he warned Molly. "Whatever you do, don't lose your concentration."

They redoubled their efforts. The cold clutched them and gnawed at them, trying to destroy their heat.

David's eyes had been closed with the effort of imagining, but after a measureless time they opened of their own accord. At first he thought he was still imagining.

Then he realised it was real. He was gazing at the surface of the stone.

Only inches from his face were the little carved symbols cut into the face of the rock. Seen up close under these conditions, suddenly he knew what they represented. There was a circle with spiky rays that could only be the sun. Other wavy vertical lines were meant to indicate fire. When David had first seen them with his father, they had been so worn it was impossible to say what they represented. But now they were as sharp and clear as if they had just been chiselled into the stone.

The glittery bits he had originally identified as mica seemed larger. As he looked, he realised they were giving off tiny pinpricks of golden light.

"Sunstone," he whispered.

"What?" Molly turned her head toward him.

"Don't," he warned her again. "Just keep concentrating."

What a sunstone might be, or who had given it that name, David could not say. Yet he was sure this *was* a sunstone, and it had certain powers. The people who erected the stone circle must have known about its powers too. They had built the circle and placed the sunstone very carefully as part of a ritual the people of David's era did not understand.

Concentrate, he reminded himself. Sun, heat, fire.

Then their voices were joined by the sound of other chanting that seemed to come from a great distance. David raised his head and peered over the sunstone. Within a white mist, a dark stone circle was gradually taking shape. Shadows moved inside the circle. The chanting grew louder.

"Who are they?" Molly breathed beside him.

"Don't be frightened," he told her. "I'm not sure they can even see us."

"But who are they, David?"

"The people who erected the stones, I think. They knew how to use the stones. They didn't just put them up to look at or pray to. They used the stones almost like some sort of machine that could do things. Manipulate the weather, maybe."

"I don't understand."

"I don't either," the boy admitted.

Glancing down, he saw a snowflake fall onto the sleeve of his denim jacket. He could not afford to stand there making guesses. The cold was trying to come back. He leaned against the stone and began his own chanting again, summoning the images of heat and sunshine and trying, with desperate faith, to believe.

As the people who erected the stones must have believed.

CHAPTER TWENTY-ONE

Molly was very tired, and the tingling sensation was becoming almost painful. It seemed as if she had been holding her hands against the grainy surface of the stone for years and years. "When can we stop, David?" she asked hoarsely.

"I don't know." He did not like the way she sounded, weak and sick. He risked turning enough to look at her. The girl's face was frighteningly pale and there was a huge bump on the side of her head that he had not noticed before. He wondered if she was going to faint.

"Are you okay?" he asked anxiously. "I need you doing this with me, Molly. I don't think I'm strong enough by myself."

"I'm okay," she replied.

They resumed chanting, but her voice grew weaker and weaker. David was about to despair when he felt a jolt almost like an electrical shock run through his body. He turned to find Molly staring back at him. "Did you feel that? What was it?"

His eyes slid past her and he gave a cry that startled them both. "Look!"

Moving her head made her wince, but when she saw what he was looking at Molly forgot her pain.

Around them stretched a field grassy with summer.

When Molly looked at David again there was sunlight on his face.

He hardly dared speak. "I think we're . . . back," he said at last. But he kept both hands on the sunstone, just in case.

Molly drew a deep, ragged breath. "Is it over then? Are we safe?"

He wanted to tell her yes, but his father had always told him lies made things worse. "I hope it's over," he said. Experimentally, he lifted one hand from the stone.

Nothing happened.

He took away his other hand.

The warm sun continued to shine on him like a blessing.

"Maybe we had best go home," he told Molly.

Dragging their feet wearily, they trudged back toward the farmhouse. David felt too tired to speak. But he was not too tired to notice and appreciate the late afternoon sunshine lying across the land in shafts of warm golden light.

When they were halfway to the house, Molly

said in a voice hoarse with fatigue, "The Ice Age, David."

"What about it?"

"You said we were sending a message . . . to the Ice Age?"

He nodded.

"How can that be?"

"Remember what I said about tapping into nature's memory?"

"I do. But I didn't understand it."

"Neither do I, Molly. Yet I'm convinced that nature's memory of the Ice Age is still in the earth, waiting to come back again. Maybe that's what climate change is, elemental memories resurfacing. Because I can communicate with this particular one somehow, I've given it a sort of gateway into here and now.

"When you and I concentrated so hard on heat and sunshine we drove it back – for a while. But the gateway's still open. And I don't know how to close it."

Molly glanced over her shoulder. "You think it's in the stone circle?"

"I think that's one gateway, but not the only one. If I'm right, wherever I've felt a . . . a *cold* place, that's where it can break through again."

"Well you certainly can't stand guard at all of them! What are you going to do?"

There was only one answer. "Tell my father, and anyone else who will listen. Try to persuade them and get them to help us."

"Will they even believe us?"

"They might think I was telling tales, but you're a witness, you were there too. If you back me up they will have to listen," he told the girl with a confidence he did not feel.

Considered while they were walking across a sunny summer field, the story sounded too bizarre. They would have a better chance of convincing people they had seen a flying saucer.

Maybe, David thought grimly, we should just forget it. But then his eye was drawn to something sparkling in one of the depressions left by the hooves of the cattle.

Unmelted by the sun, a crescent of ice sparkled like a warning.

When they reached the house, Mr. Doyle opened the kitchen door and stood framed in the doorway waiting for them. He seemed surprised to notice the direction from which they came. "I thought you were over at David's," was his greeting to Molly.

"I didn't make it," she said.

He gave his daughter a hard look. "What's happened to you, lass? And what's that bump . . . " He caught her by the shoulder and turned her toward the westering sunlight. "You've hit your head a terrible blow! How did that happen? David?"

"David wasn't there," Molly said. "I fell off my bike when the storm started. Then afterwards I went to find him . . . and here we are."

Suddenly the girl swayed on her feet. Liam Doyle caught her before she could fall and scooped her into his arms. Ignoring David or anything else but his daughter, he carried Molly up the stairs and into her bedroom.

David followed him anxiously.

Molly's was the dormer bedroom, with wallpaper sprigged with bright yellow flowers and a yellow coverlet on the bed. It was a bright, cheerful room, and it looked like her, David thought.

But she was not bright and cheerful now. She lay very small and still on the yellow coverlet while her father bent over her. "This girl could have a concussion," he said. "I'm going to phone the doctor."

To his relief, the phone lines were still intact after the storm and the doctor promised to come at once. David wanted to wait with Molly, but Mr. Doyle insisted he go down and wait in the kitchen with the other men.

"Or perhaps you should go home, lad," he added. "Will your parents not be worried about you?"

"I can't go until I know Molly's all right."

"No, no of course not. Well, you wait here then. If she asks for you I'll call you."

In the kitchen the Aga was radiating warmth and the two farm helpers were talking about the freak storm. As David entered the room one was

126

saying, "Weather's changing all over the globe, y'know. We're lucky to be in Ireland. Other places are having it much worse with drought and earthquakes and . . ."

His companion nodded. "It's all that atomic testing they did in the fifties."

"Not at all. My old Mam says it's a visitation of God upon us for our wickedness," the first man replied with conviction.

David looked from one to the other. Were their theories any more unlikely than his own?

He went over to the Aga and stood as close as he could to the stove, the squat and cheerful iron monster that could banish the cold.

But though the kitchen was warm, the cold remained in his bones.

CHAPTER TWENTY-TWO

The doctor confirmed that Molly had a mild concussion. He said she would be just fine, but he wanted to take her to the regional hospital for X-rays and to stay overnight for observation, and Mr. Doyle agreed. David wanted to go with them but Molly's father would not hear of it. "You go on home, lad, there's nothing more you can do for her. She's going to be all right, the doctor said so. I'll call to you tomorrow and let you know how she's doing."

When he got home he found both his parents waiting for him. By the heaviness of the air he knew that they had been arguing again, but when he entered the cottage they met him with relieved expressions. "I was so worried about you," his mother began before he had his jacket off.

"I was fine, Mom; really. I just went over to the Doyles'."

"You look exhausted. Did you get caught in that dreadful storm?"

"It was Molly who got caught," he said. "The wind blew her off her bicycle and she hit her head. They've taken her to hospital."

"Oh that poor girl!" Alice McHugh's eyes mirrored her sympathy. "Is there anything we can do?" she asked quickly.

David was satisfied that he had diverted his mother's attention, but he could feel his father looking at him speculatively.

Mrs. McHugh prepared a hot meal and they sat down at the kitchen table to eat, but David could hardly keep his eyes open. Before dessert, he excused himself and went off to bed.

The small bedroom was very quiet. He sank gratefully onto his bed and was almost asleep when he heard the door creak open. Then his father's weight sagged one side of the bed.

"What happened today, David?" he asked softly.

The boy kept his eyes closed. "I told you. Molly fell off her bike and . . ."

"What happened to *you*? There was more than you told us, wasn't there?"

He could not lie. "There was."

"You had best tell me."

He knew that tone. His father was much quieter than his mother, but when his voice was very soft it meant business.

David dragged himself upright in the bed and bunched his pillows behind his back. Arthur McHugh waited until his son was comfortable, then reached over to the bedside locker and picked up a cup of hot cocoa he had brought in with him. "Drink this," he advised David.

The cocoa tasted good and helped clear his brain a little. "I guess, well, Molly and I both got caught in the storm," he began.

"Why were you out in it at all? I thought you had better sense, David, especially after the last few days."

David met his father's eyes. "I guess I'd better begin at the beginning," he said.

Professor McHugh listened without comment as David described his visit with Molly to the ring fort and the things that had happened to him there, and afterward. He told about his experiences at the stone circle, describing both what he had felt and what he had seen. He tried in spite of his weariness to sound rational and thoughtful, but the more he talked, the more foolish he felt.

Who would ever believe such a wild tale?

At last he ran out of words and sat huddled in the bed, gazing at his father through bleary eyes.

Arthur McHugh drew a deep breath.

"Is that all? You're sure you told me everything?"

"Yes sir."

"I know you've always had a vivid imagination, David. But if you ever want to become an archaeologist . . . " He broke off. "But that's my dream, isn't it? Like this is a dream of yours?"

"This is not a dream," David insisted. "It all happened. Molly was there, she can tell you."

"Molly has a head injury, you said so yourself. People with head injuries don't make the most reliable witnesses."

"She only got the injury today. Before then . . ."

"Yes. Before then." Professor McHugh stared very seriously at his son. "I cannot deny you have a highly unusual sensitivity to certain influences. Coupled with your imagination, that could . . ."

"I wasn't imagining!" David exclaimed. He was embarrassed to feel his eyes burning with tears. If he was not so tired he would never have cried. "It's real, it's all real. The thing in the earth, and the ice, and the glacier . . . and those people who built the stone circle and invented rituals to hold back the cold . . . it's all real, don't you see? You've spent your lifetime studying the past, Dad. Do you not believe there's more to it than bones and artefacts? Ancient people must have known many things we've forgotten about. They had to try to control the weather, because they were so vulnerable to it. All their rituals must have been bound up with their survival."

A strange, listening expression flickered across his father's face. "You know, I have read studies which demonstrate that apple trees bear more fruit in proximity to standing stones . . ."

"See!"

"What I see, David, is an overwrought boy who

is far too tired," Arthur McHugh said briskly. "I promise you I won't dismiss this theory of yours, I'll give it some serious thought, no matter how wild it sounds. But you have to promise me you'll sleep. In the morning when we're both more clear-headed we can talk again."

David felt an overwhelming sense of relief. Perhaps his father *would* listen to him! His father knew a lot of scientists; if he believed David he could convince others. With their total knowledge they could somehow . . .

He was asleep before he knew it.

No glaciers glittered in his dreams. No cold wind blew. He lay in the soft warm dark while his parents kept watch, and everything was going to be all right in the morning.

In the morning he awoke to the sound of them shouting at each other. At least his mother was shouting. But his father's voice was raised too, and clearly angry.

"My son is not a liar!"

"You're twisting my words around," Alice McHugh retorted. "I just said his story was bizarre, and no normal youngster would . . ."

"Now you're saying he's emotionally disturbed?"

"Well something's wrong with him. Surely you can see that for yourself, Arthur. He was perfectly all right until you started taking him around to those old ruins and filling his head with your nonsense."

"Archaeology is not nonsense, it is a science. And I didn't give him his ideas, he came up with them all by himself. All I did was encourage a very remarkable talent..."

David got out of bed and went to the door. He opened it just a crack. He wanted to shout at them, "Don't fight! Don't fight over me!" But he was not sure they were fighting over him.

He heard his mother's quick step bustling about the cottage, opening and closing drawers and presses. "I'm taking David back to Dublin," she said curtly, "and that's an end to it. If he stays down here any longer, who knows what wild notions he may get in his head?"

"What about me, Alice?" David's father asked. His voice was very soft again.

"I can't do anything about the notions in your head and I'm through trying," she replied. She did not sound angry any more, just very tired. "I'm through, full stop."

As surely as he recognised cold places, David knew this was the end of his parents' being together. Something had died which would not come back to life no matter how much he wished otherwise. He could hold back the cold – for a while – but he could not prevent change.

Leaving the door ajar, he went back and sat down on his bed. He propped his elbows on his knees and buried his head in his hands. The world was falling apart and he could not go to his parents for comfort because they were part of the problem.

But if the ice came back it wouldn't matter.

Nothing would matter.

So there were things more important than whether or not his parents stayed together, David told himself. Either way, life would go on.

As long as the ice did not come back.

He sat in his room for a long time, listening to the sounds beyond the door.

At last he heard his father go out and start the car and drive away. But still he stayed in his room. He did not feel like facing his mother. He heard her dragging the suitcases down from the shelf in the hall. When her footsteps approached his door he quickly lay back down and pretended to be asleep.

"David?" she whispered.

He did not move.

She went out back and began taking some clothes off the clothesline. While she was outside David slipped on his shoes, grabbed his jacket and left the cottage by the front door.

CHAPTER TWENTY-THREE

Blue sky and sunshine awaited him. To the south was a bank of puffy white clouds, beautiful and harmless.

They did not look like they carried snow.

The air was warm and did not smell of ice.

David thought of going over to the Doyles' to ask about Molly, then recalled that Mr Doyle had promised to call by with news. Better stay close to the cottage and wait for him.

The boy strolled a short distance down the narrow laneway, sniffing the fragrance of the golden gorse that billowed on either side. It had a sunny, summery smell. There was no residue of ice to be seen, even in the shadows underneath the bushes. But he was not reassured. He might go around the next bend in the road and find snowdrifts there. Everything was unstable, changing . . .

Everything was changing, unstable. In the dark earth, the spirit of the ice felt the ponderous movement of geologic time. The planet was beginning a new cycle.

The kingdom of the cold was coming around again.

Like a giant shuddering its way out of sleep, the spirit gathered its forces. Sending out invisible feelers almost like thoughts, it searched for the warm one. The warm one who opened the gateways.

Eons had passed since the last time the force in the earth encountered beings sensitive to itself. Once there had been whole tribes of warm ones who were aware of its presence. Some offered sacrifices out of fear; others created elaborate rituals of protection. They had erected barriers which, once the rituals were no longer practised, could also serve as gateways. All that was required was a new and different ritual. But for that more warm ones were needed.

And so the spirit in the ice had waited. At last its patience was rewarded with the discovery of a new warm one who sensed its power. The new warm one was not a whole tribe with powerful combined energies, however. This warm one was solitary, or almost solitary, and small. Such a being should be helpless and easy to control.

Instead, the warm one had proved to be very difficult. Each time the spirit of the ice touched the small living spark the creature fought back. Instead of welcoming the elemental being as a god, the warm one had attacked with darts of heat and brightness.

But the spirit of the ice was not discouraged. It could not experience such emotions. It could only try again, obedient to a cycle as old as the planet itself.

Try. Reach out. Insert itself into a human mind, force itself through a gateway in space and time. Return. Reclaim.

There. The warm one. Moving. Not close to a gateway yet, but irresistibly drawn.

Slouching along the laneway, David kept listening for a car. Either his father returning or Mr. Doyle with news of Molly, he didn't care which. He just wanted somebody . . . Then he realised the day had gone very quiet. When he first came outside there had been birds singing. Now there was no sound except the faraway whoosh of the wind.

Rising wind.

Oh no! the boy thought in horror. *Not again.*

He turned to go back to the cottage, but before he had taken more than a few steps he felt a tug like a powerful magnetic force, pulling at him. Drawing him away from the cottage, dragging him between two prickly gorse bushes, leading him down a tiny pathway he had never noticed before.

David was powerless to control his own feet. That was the most frightening of all.

Carrying him against his will, they walked along the pathway until it opened out to reveal a small clearing in the gorse. Most of the clearing was taken up by a tumble of dark grey stones. When David looked closer he saw what had once been a dolmen, ruined now by time or vandals. It was so well-concealed by the gorse that a person on the lane twenty yards away could never have seen it. Probably no one knew it was there.

Probably no one knew about the cold place, either – until David stepped into its centre and gasped in shock. The air around him became an icy bath, freezing the marrow in his bones. There was no snow, no sleet, only the intense and invisible cold radiating up from the ground.

The experience was different from that of the stone circle, or the ring fort. Instead of covering a large space, here the phenomenon seemed limited to the small area of cold in which David stood. Everything else looked perfectly normal. It was as if something were focusing all its attention on that one spot.

David tried to back away. He found he could lift his foot and move his leg; he was not totally captive. Strangely, the discovery gave him more courage. He stopped trying to get away. It would be childish to run. He wasn't being hurt, was he? He was simply . . . cold. There wasn't even any glacier around him. He could still see the golden gorse blooming and the sun shining. There was no danger. Just a cold place.

David swallowed hard. The adult thing to do – the thing his father would surely do – would be to stay and investigate.

Investigate the Unknown. He whispered the word to himself as he had done once before, savouring the sound. The marvellous, mysterious Unknown, that had reached out and touched him of all people.

He *would* not be afraid.

Slowly he bent his knees until he was crouching on the earth. Without knowing why he did so, he reached out his left hand and laid his palm flat on the bare ground.

CHAPTER TWENTY-FOUR

Below him in the earth, the spirit of the ice felt that tiny touch of heat. Before, it had reacted with a flood of its own cold, an overwhelming rush as it sought to break free. But though elemental spirits had no emotions as humans know emotion, it had intelligence of a sort. It could learn. This time it would not be over-eager and stimulate the warm one to fight back.

There was time.

All the time in the world.

With infinite delicacy, the cold crept upward.

As he crouched with his hand flat on the ground, David felt a new sensation creep over him. He was still cold, but the cold had ceased to be unpleasant. It was . . . fresh, and crisp, and purifying. It was sweeter than the overpowering, cloying perfume of the gorse. He stopped shivering. He felt strangely invigorated, as if he had been touched by a sea breeze on a hot July afternoon.

Beneath his palm the soil was firm and cool.

David looked around. For the first time, he noticed that the quality of the sunlight was beginning to change. It slanted across the land with the hint of subdued gold which heralds the approach of autumn. The dark green of the gorse stems held hints of russet. The weeds around the tumbled dolmen were beginning to turn yellowish and brittle.

A new season, thought David. Everything's going to be different now.

He was not sure what he meant. But he resolved not to be afraid.

Maybe the Ice Age was going to come back. Not today or tomorrow, it could not possibly happen that fast. But it could happen, as the last few days had shown.

And if the weather was going to change that drastically, people would need to be prepared. They would need scientists who were imaginative enough to study the past in order to learn ways of dealing with the cold. Scientists who were not afraid of new ideas – or of old ones.

Slowly, David stood up. He found he was reluctant to take his hand away from the cool, bare earth. When he was erect again he held his fingers to his nose and took a deep sniff.

They smelled of ice.

With his head down in thought, he walked back toward the cottage. The cold place made no attempt to hold him. Once he paused and turned around, but he could no longer see the tumble of dark stones.

Yet he knew they were there.

Perhaps there were cold places everywhere, not just in Ireland.

It would take a while yet, David was thinking, but the years of childhood were drawing to a close. Summer was almost over. He would return to school, study, pass his Leaving, go to university, study more . . . he would become a man.

Meanwhile his parents would pass through their own seasons. They might not choose to share the future but it was their choice to make. Their lives belonged to them as surely as his belonged to him. Change would come to all of them.

What had Molly said? "Everything changes, it has to. That's nature's way."

David kicked at a sparkling pebble on the path. It might have been there for years. Now it was knocked aside into the gorse, and for that pebble everything was different.

Molly, he thought as he walked back in the direction of the cottage. He hoped they would let her out of hospital today. He would like to be able to see her before his mother took him back to Dublin. He had so much to tell her. But he could always write; maybe putting down his thoughts in a letter would make them more clear in his own mind. Maybe some time she could come up to

Dublin and he could show her the city and discuss his plans with her . . .

. . . plans that were already beginning to take shape in his head, like a sudden inspiration.

When he was grown, he would go in search of other cold places around the world. He would photograph them, document them, see if any others had sunstones. If there were sunstones elsewhere, it would mean more than one group of ancient people had rituals for controlling the weather.

It would mean that in some ways Stone Age people were more advanced than modern people who could not control the weather.

David felt a sense of excitement growing in him. There was so much to be discovered! He might become an archaeologist; that would please his father. Or a meteorologist, studying the climate. There were a lot of ways to go . . .

Suddenly he found himself hurrying back toward the cottage. There were many changes coming but he was not afraid. He was in a hurry for the future.

CHAPTER TWENTY-FIVE

Deep in the earth, the spirit of the ice waited. The careful, probing contact with the warm one had been most rewarding. Warm ones possessed the gift of movement. This latest warm one would travel far away, carrying with it an awareness of the cold. Of the ice. An awareness which would touch other spirits sleeping in other, distant lands, and summon them to awaken.

It would take a while yet, but the Age of Ice would gather its allies and return to claim its kingdom. Meanwhile the spirit in the earth waited. It had time.

All the time in the world.